SPELLBINDER

The Spellbinder series
as seen on TV

SPELLBINDER

Paul's World
BOOK II

Mark Shirrefs AND **John Thomson**

*Hodder
Children's
Books*

a division of Hodder Headline plc

Copyright © Film Australia 1995

Adapted from the television series *Spellbinder*, a Film Australia/
Telewizja Polska production with assistance from the Nine Network
Australia, financed by the Australian Film Finance Corporation.
Series produced by Noel Price. Series devised by Ron Saunders.

First published in Australia and New Zealand 1995
by Hodder Headline Australia Pty Ltd

First published in Great Britain in 1996
by Hodder Children's Books

The rights of Mark Shirrefs and John Thomson to be identified as the
Authors of the Work have been asserted by them in accordance with
the Copyright, Designs and Patents Act 1988.

10 9 8 7 6 5 4 3 2 1

A Catalogue record for this book is available from the British
Library

ISBN 0 340 66738 9

Typeset by Avon Dataset Ltd, Bidford on Avon, Warwickshire

Printed and bound in Great Britain by
Cox & Wyman Ltd, Reading, Berks.

Hodder Children's Books
a division of Hodder Headline plc
338 Euston Road
London NW1 3BH

Contents

Prologue

Paul Reynolds leaned back against the rocks by the cave and let out a huge sigh of relief. He was home. He had escaped from the ruthless Spellbinder, Ashka, and the doorway to her parallel world was closed. Paul smiled as he imagined how angry she must be that he had got away. Without his knowledge of gunpowder, Ashka would never be able to take control of her world.

Paul's only regret was that he had not been able to save his friend, Correon, who had been banished to the Wastelands: there was little chance that the old Spellbinder would have survived that harsh, waterless place.

Paul shook the thought from his mind and turned to watch his best friend, Alex, dancing around like an idiot with Katrina. Without their help, he would never have got back to this world. Paul was amazed that Alex would have anything to do with Katrina: Alex had always thought that she was the biggest nerd at their school. A lot must have changed while he was away.

Now the most important thing was to get home and let his family know he was alive. Paul wondered how his father would react when he introduced Riana and explained that she was from a parallel world.

Paul's reverie was broken by an anguished cry. Riana was staring at the place where the doorway to her world had been. Paul went over and put his hand on her shoulder. Riana turned and Paul saw tears brimming in her eyes.

'I can't stay here,' she cried. 'I have to go back!'

Lost and Found

'Calm down,' Paul said gently. 'We'll find a way to get the doorway open again.'

'How?' Riana asked anxiously. The Summoning Tower in her world had been damaged in Paul's fight with Ashka. Without it, the doorway could not be opened.

'My father's a scientist,' Paul reassured her. 'He's a genius. He'll figure out a way.'

'Are you sure?'

'I promise.' Paul looked at the Spellbinder power suit he was wearing and smiled. 'I can't wait to see his face when he sees this.'

'What is that?' Katrina asked, peering at the heavy black jacket studded with copper cables and elaborate fittings.

'A power suit. The Spellbinders use it to control their people. It throws electro-magnetic power-bolts.'

'Wild,' Alex said. 'Give us a demo.'

Paul struck his wrists together to energise the suit. The copper plates touched but no spark flashed between them. He tried again and then looked apologetically at Alex. 'The powerstones must be dead.'

Paul twisted to unbuckle the power suit and cried out in pain as the thick leather tore the skin over his stomach. He looked down and saw that a hole had been burnt in the suit. Blistered flesh was visible beneath it.

'Nasty burn,' Alex said. 'How'd you get it?'

'Ashka hit me with a power-bolt. Riana, help me get this off. We've got to let Dad know I'm safe.'

'What if the doorway opens while we're gone?' Riana asked as she helped with the suit.

'Yeah,' Alex said, looking nervously at the cave. 'This Ashka character might come through.'

'We'll make sure she can't,' Paul said. 'Alex, pull the cable down.'

Alex went to the cave mouth and unfastened the steel cable he had stolen from his mother's washing line. It was still warm from carrying the electricity that had opened the door to the Spellbinders' world. Alex nervously glanced up at the high-tension power lines above the tree to which the other end of the cable was tied. He hurried across to the tree and dropped the coiled cable behind the trunk.

'Now you've got a chance to see my world,' Paul told Riana. 'You can watch TV and eat your first pizza and find out what a hot shower feels like. You'll love it.'

Riana didn't look very excited.

'Don't worry, Riana,' Katrina said cheerily. 'You'll be safe with us.'

'But what about my family?'

Katrina didn't know what to say. Riana looked away. With the doorway closed, there was no way of knowing what was happening in the Spellbinders' world.

In the Clayhill barn, Riana's family were hurriedly loading a sled with supplies.

'Why do we have to leave Clayhill?' Arla, Riana's sister, asked.

3

'The Spellbinder Ashka is angry with us,' her father replied. 'But once I show the pictures in this box to the Regents, we will be safe from her.'

Bron carefully stowed Paul's video-camera in a leather bag on the sled. He didn't understand how the pictures of Ashka and her Apprentice Gryvon had got into the box but he had seen them and heard Ashka plotting to overthrow the Regents.

'We can't go without Riana,' Arla protested.

Jal, Riana's little brother, started to sob and Maran gave the boy a hug. 'It's alright, Jal. Riana will find us.'

'I'll get Correon's magic stones,' Arla said. In the rush to get away, the little magnetic balls the old Spellbinder had given Jal, had been left in the cottage. They were Jal's most precious possessions. She headed for the door but her mother grabbed her arm. 'No, Arla.'

'But Correon said they'd keep us all safe.'

'There's no time. We'll get them when we come back.'

Maran went to help Bron finish loading.

While their backs were turned, Arla slipped out of the barn.

As Arla ran towards her cottage, Ashka and Gryvon tramped into the village square. Ashka's normally gleaming power suit was covered in mud and she did not look happy. Arla flattened herself out of sight against the side-wall of her home as the front door opened and the Summoner staggered out.

'Spellbinder, forgive me,' he stammered, dropping to his knees. 'We were tricked. Riana's mother put sleeping draught in our tea ... the boy escaped. We might still catch him.'

'It's too late,' Ashka snapped. 'He's gone back to his own world and taken the girl with him.'

'Where's Riana's family, Father?' Gryvon asked.

'I don't know.'

'Find them,' Ashka shouted. 'They have an object belonging to the boy. A black box. If it is not found and brought to me, everyone in this village will suffer.'

The Summoner was shocked by her threat. Ashka strode away. Gryvon avoided his

5

father's eyes and went after her.

'You men,' the Summoner called to three watching villagers, 'search the village for Bron's family.'

Arla raced back to the barn.

'Where have you been?' Maran cried as she burst through the door.

'I went home to get the magic stones,' Arla panted, 'but the Spellbinder was there. She said Paul took Riana to his world. The Spellbinder wants Paul's picture box. She told the Summoner to find us.'

Bron peered out of the door and saw the men heading towards the barn. 'Maran, take Jal and Arla up to the loft and hide.' He took the bag containing the camera from the sled.

'What are you doing?' Maran asked.

'If they want this so badly, maybe they'll chase me for it. Stay hidden till it's safe, then take the children to the forest.'

'What about Riana?' Arla pleaded.

'I'm sure Paul will look after her. Now do as I say.'

Maran opened her mouth to protest but

Bron kissed her and bolted out of the barn.

'There he is,' the Summoner cried as Bron ran towards the trees at the edge of the village holding the camera in his hand. 'He's got the picture box.'

Ashka and Gryvon came running.

'Stop!' Ashka yelled. She struck her wrists together to energise her power suit but only a weak spark jumped between them. 'The powerstone is depleted,' she snarled. 'Don't just stand there.'

The Summoner and his men took off after Bron.

'Make sure they find him,' Ashka snapped at Gryvon.

The Apprentice raced after his father.

Paul, Alex and Katrina trudged along the edge of the dusty country road. Riana walked a few paces behind them, trying not to think about her family.

'Look, guys,' Paul said quietly. 'I think we'd better keep this whole thing a secret—at least until I've had a chance to talk to my dad.'

'But what am I going to tell my parents?' Katrina asked. 'I sneaked out to come up here.'

'The worst that can happen is you'll get grounded. If people find out about Riana, she might never be allowed to go home.'

'OK,' Katrina said reluctantly, 'I won't say anything.'

'Me neither,' Alex added.

'Thanks. I really owe you guys a lot.'

They reached the top of a hill. Riana caught up with them and stopped, gaping in amazement. The hill provided a breathtaking view of the suburbs of Sydney. Red-tiled roofs and straight black roads seemed to go on forever. Just visible in the distance, the tall glass towers of the city gleamed in the sun. They made the Spellbinders' castle seem tiny.

'That's Sydney,' Paul said to Riana. 'Big, isn't it?'

'How many people live there?' the stunned girl asked.

'Millions.'

'How many is that?'

'More than you've ever dreamed of.' Paul smiled sadly. 'I wish Correon could have seen this.'

The road eventually led the foursome into a small country town.

'There's another car,' Riana cried, pointing at a battered sedan.

'When we get home, you can go for a drive in my dad's car,' Paul promised.

He led the way towards an old, bluestone railway station. On a notice board was a missing person's poster with Paul's photograph.

'Paul, it's you,' Riana said.

'Your dad put them up,' Alex explained.

'What do the words say?' Riana asked.

'That Paul's missing.' Katrina pointed to the printing under the picture. 'That's his name: Paul Reynolds.'

'I don't want anyone to recognise me.' Paul ripped the poster off the wall and threw it in a bin. 'Come on.'

'What is this place?' Riana asked Paul as she looked around the platform.

'A railway station. We're going to catch a train. Has anybody got money for tickets?'

Katrina shook her head.

'I'll get them,' Alex grumbled. 'But I'm keeping a list of my expenses.'

He headed for the ticket office.

'What's a train?' Riana asked, peering over the edge of the platform at the shining steel rails.

Paul grinned. 'Wait and see.'

'It's wonderful,' Riana screeched with delight, her face pressed to the window of the train carriage. Outside, the countryside sped past at eighty kilometres an hour. Paul smiled, relieved that Riana's anxiety had lifted.

'Hello,' she said to a man sitting across from her. 'I'm Riana and this is Paul. He's going to take me for a ride in a car. His father's got one.'

The man took refuge behind his newspaper. Alex grinned at Paul and Katrina. 'She's great.'

The train pulled into Sydney Central station and Riana watched with amazement as the carriage doors automatically slid open.

'Is your house near here?' she asked Paul.

'No, we have to take another train to get there.'

'Good. I like trains.'

Riana followed Paul, Alex and Katrina through the busy station. It was bigger than the marketplace in Rivertown. Riana couldn't stop staring at the strange clothes and faces. There was a sudden roar in the air and Riana looked up.

'Paul, look!' she cried, stopping to gape at the silver airliner that was climbing into the sky from the nearby airport.

'It's an aeroplane,' Paul explained. There was a whistle from the next platform. 'Come on.'

Riana followed Paul as he hurried after Katrina and Alex towards the waiting train. She looked up again at the plane and collided with a corpulent businessman carrying an armful of files. Manila folders and papers scattered over the platform.

Paul, Alex and Katrina jumped onto the train. Riana started to go after them but the man grabbed her arm.

'Let me go,' Riana yelled, struggling to break free of his sweaty grasp. The train doors shut.

'Not until you help me pick these up,' the man growled, pointing to the folders on the ground.

Riana bent to pick them up and the man loosened his grip. Riana broke free. As she ran towards the train, it started to move. 'Paul,' she yelled, hammering on the window.

Paul tried to force the doors open but they wouldn't budge. The train gathered speed. Riana ran after it but was stopped by a metal barrier at the end of the platform. As the train drew out of the station, Riana started to climb down onto the tracks to follow it.

'No you don't,' a station attendant yelled and pulled Riana back onto the platform. 'Show me your ticket.'

'I don't know what a ticket is,' Riana protested, watching the train disappear.

'Don't get smart,' the attendant snapped. 'If you haven't got a ticket, you'll have to buy one.'

He started to haul the frightened girl towards the office. Riana twisted out of his grasp, ran back along the platform and disappeared into the crowd leaving the station.

Outside, she stumbled through some roadworks and onto the busy street. A truck sounded its air-horn. The deafening noise made Riana jump back. She fell against a parked car and its burglar alarm went off. The air was filled with a piercing wail.

'Get away from there!' someone yelled.

Riana saw an angry man running towards her. She turned and fled along the street.

A train pulled into Central station and Paul, Alex and Katrina leaped out of the carriage onto the platform.

'Riana,' Paul shouted, but there was no answer. He handed the power suit to Alex. 'Stay here in case she comes back. Katrina, check the other platforms. I'll look outside.'

Paul hurried out of the station and looked around. 'Riana, Riana!'

There was no reply. Angry with himself for losing her, Paul kicked over a traffic barrier around the roadworks.

'Hey! What's your problem?' a young police constable shouted.

'Did you see a girl come out of the station a

while ago?' Paul asked him. 'She's blond, my age, wearing green shorts.'

'No,' the constable said. 'Why? Is she lost?'

'Yes. She doesn't know this worl ... city. She's foreign ... from Iceland.'

The constable reached for his radio. 'I'll put out a call. What's her name?'

'Riana.'

'Riana who?'

Paul realised it was going to be too hard to explain about Riana. 'Don't worry about it. I'll find her.' He started back towards the station entrance.

'Hang on.' Paul looked round and saw the constable pointing to the barrier he had kicked over. 'Pick that up.'

As Paul bent to pick it up, he groaned in pain and clutched his stomach. The constable hurried over. 'Are you hurt?'

'I'm fine,' Paul said, gritting his teeth.

The constable lifted Paul's hand from his stomach. 'That's a bad burn. How did you get it?'

'It's nothing,' Paul insisted.

'What's your name?'

Paul started to move away but the constable took his arm. 'I'd think you'd better come with me.' He led Paul towards his car.

Katrina and Alex hurried out of the station and looked around. They watched in dismay as the police car drove away with Paul inside.

'I found this kid near Central,' the constable said as he helped Paul into the police station. 'Won't tell me his name. He's got a bad burn. I think he might be a runaway.'

The female sergeant behind the desk took one look at Paul then pointed to the missing person poster on the notice board. 'He's Paul Reynolds. The boy who's been missing in the bush.'

The constable stared at the poster then at Paul. 'Why didn't you say so? Your family must be worried sick. Do they know you're OK?'

'Not yet. But I have to find Riana.'

'You just take it easy,' the constable said. 'We'll find her. That's our job. I'll take down her details.' He sat Paul down on a bench.

'What say I call a doctor then give your father a ring?' the sergeant suggested.

Paul nodded, too exhausted to argue.

Riana looked desperately through the wire mesh fence at the empty railway tracks. She realised it was hopeless. Trains travelled fast and Paul would be far away by now. She turned back to the street, which was filled with crowds of daytime shoppers.

'Can you tell me where a boy called Paul lives?' Riana asked a passing man.

'Paul who?'

'Paul. His father's a scientist. He's got a sister called Christine.'

The man looked warily at her. 'Where are you from?'

'... I can't tell you.'

The man hurried away.

'Can you help me?' she asked a young woman. 'I'm looking for a boy.'

'Don't waste your time,' the woman muttered. 'They're not worth the pain.' She walked on.

Crowds of people were hurrying by, many

more than Riana had ever seen. No-one took any notice of the confused and frightened girl. Looking up at the towering buildings, Riana felt as though she was trapped in a vast canyon. She huddled against a wall, wondering how she was ever going to find Paul.

Paul sat impatiently beside the constable, who was carefully filling out an interview form.

'So Riana's got fair hair, green eyes and she's from Iceland.' The constable smiled wistfully. 'I've always wanted to visit there. It sounds fascinating.'

'This is wasting time,' Paul moaned. 'Can't you go out and look for her?'

'Take it easy, Paul.' The sergeant handed him a mug of tea. 'Constable Mullet will fax her description straight through and they'll put out a bulletin. Drink your tea.'

She gestured to the constable, who got up and went behind the desk. The sergeant sat down. 'Now, Paul, would you like to tell me where you've been all this time?'

'I'd rather wait for my dad.'

Paul looked up as a distinguished-looking man came into the station carrying a black bag. The sergeant beckoned him over. 'Paul, this is Dr Macallum.'

'I don't need a doctor,' Paul protested.

'You've been missing for two weeks,' the sergeant said. 'We have to make sure you're alright. And that burn needs treatment.'

'Is there somewhere I can do an examination?' the doctor asked.

'The interview room's free.' The sergeant motioned for the constable to help Paul into the room, then began to explain the situation to the doctor.

Paul sat on a hard wooden chair in the small interview room while the doctor carefully applied a dressing to his stomach.

'This burn looks electrical,' he said. 'How did you get it?'

'I ... um ... I don't remember.'

'Do you recall how you got lost in the first place?'

'No. It's all a blank.'

The doctor shone a pencil torch into Paul's

eyes. 'Well, you're not in bad shape for someone who's been lost in the bush for so long.' He turned off the torch and put it in his pocket. 'So who's this girl Riana?'

'I ... I met her in the bush,' Paul stammered. 'She's from Iceland. She looked after me.'

'So you can remember some things?'

'I guess so.'

'Was Riana pretty?'

'What's that got to do with anything?' Paul snapped.

'Take it easy, Paul.'

There was a knock on the door and the sergeant opened it. Behind her were Paul's father, Brian, and his sister, Christine. Christine ran to Paul and threw her arms around him.

'I was starting to think I'd never see you again,' a relieved Brian said as he joined in the hug. 'Where were you?' He noticed the dressing on Paul's stomach and looked anxiously at the doctor.

'Don't worry, Mr Reynolds,' the doctor said. 'It's just a minor burn. Paul can go home. If I could just have a word?'

'Christine, wait outside with Paul. I'll be out

in a sec.' Brian gave Paul another hug, then Christine took her brother's hand and pulled him out of the room. Brian looked at the doctor. 'Is Paul alright?'

'Apart from exhaustion and a slight case of amnesia.'

'Amnesia?'

'He doesn't seem to remember what happened to him,' the doctor said. 'That's made him anxious—and the exhausted mind plays funny tricks.'

'What do you mean?'

'Paul believes he was rescued by a pretty girl from Iceland.'

'Iceland? Why Iceland?'

'He was probably cold,' the doctor suggested. 'Look, my guess is he just needs to rest. Hopefully, after a good night's sleep, he'll remember everything. My advice is to humour him. Just go along with whatever he says.'

'Why did you run away?' Christine asked Paul as they waited in the foyer of the police station. 'Dad's been out of his mind. So have I.'

'I didn't run away,' Paul said.

'Then where were you?'

Paul noticed that the sergeant at the desk was listening. 'I don't remember. I missed you.'

'How do you know, if you can't remember anything?'

Paul laughed at Christine's logic. Brian and Dr Macallum came out of the interview room.

'Can I take my son home now?' Brian asked the sergeant.

'Of course. We'll come around for a statement when he's feeling better.'

'What about Riana?' Paul asked.

Brian looked curiously at him. 'Who's Riana?'

'The girl that helped me. She's lost.'

'Don't worry,' the sergeant said. 'We'll let you know if we find her.'

Brian and Christine put their arms around Paul and helped him out of the station.

'Dad,' Paul said when they were on the street, 'I told the doctor I couldn't remember what happened to me but I really can.'

'That's terrific. Do you want to tell me about it?'

'I wasn't lost. I got blasted into another

world. It's run by weird scientists called Spellbinders.' Paul waited eagerly for his father's response but Brian just stared at him. 'Truly, Dad. They live in a huge castle ...'

'A castle?' Christine asked.

'Tell me the rest in the car,' Brian said quickly. 'I'll bet you could do with a bath. And some clean clothes. Where did you get these?'

'They belonged to Riana's father. Riana saved my life and looked after me.' Brian opened the back door of his car and Paul climbed in. 'Her family live in a village called Clayhill. They don't have cars or TV or shops.'

Brian started the car and drove off.

'Do the Spellbinders really live in a castle?' Christine asked excitedly.

'Yeah. But once you go in you can never come out. If it wasn't for Riana, I'd still be trapped there.'

Through the rear-view mirror, Brian watched his son with mounting concern.

'What do you reckon Paul told the police?'

Katrina asked as she and Alex walked homewards from the railway station.

'Who knows?' Alex replied, shifting the heavy power suit under his other arm. 'But we'd better stay quiet until we see him.'

A silver Volvo station wagon screeched to a halt beside them. 'Katrina,' Mrs Muggleton yelled out of the car window, 'we've been worried sick.'

Mr Muggleton got out and stormed round to his daughter. 'Where have you been?'

Katrina looked at Alex, who quickly shook his head. 'I've ... just been hanging around with Alex.'

'You were strictly forbidden to see him,' Mr Muggleton thundered. 'Weren't you?'

'Yes, Dad.'

'Get in the car!'

Katrina quickly did as she was told. Mr Muggleton glared at Alex. 'I don't want you coming near Katrina again.'

He got back in the car, slammed the door and roared away.

Alex groaned. How could things go so wrong so fast?

Brian and Christine stood in the loungeroom, watching Paul devour a bowl of steaming vegetable soup.

'Does it taste alright?' Christine asked anxiously. While Paul was away, she had learned how to make soup out of a can.

'It's fine. Not quite as good as the soup Riana's mum makes. She uses vegetables right out of her garden.'

'Does Riana have any sisters or brothers?'

Paul stifled a yawn.

'Let Paul eat in peace, Christine,' Brian said. 'You can help me make some dessert.'

Christine followed her father into the kitchen. 'Darling, Paul's had a very difficult time,' Brian said quietly. 'You mustn't believe everything he says.'

'Aren't the Spellbinders true?'

'Paul thinks they are and that's all that matters. He needs to rest before we can find out what really happened. Now go and see if he wants some more soup.'

Christine went out and Brian collapsed in a chair.

'Dad!' Christine yelled.

Fearing some new calamity, Brian leaped up and raced into the dining room. Paul was fast asleep with his head on the table, the soup spoon still in his hand.

Alex was in his garage, looking for somewhere to hide the bulky power suit when his older brother, Nick, appeared in the doorway. 'Where have you been all day?'

Alex quickly threw an old blanket over the suit and smiled innocently, but Nick marched over and uncovered it. 'What's that?' he asked.

'That? Well ... I guess you had to find out some time.' Alex puffed out his chest and spoke in a deep voice. 'I'm not really your brother. I'm Electroman—the mutated product of a genetic engineering experiment that went wrong.'

'Mutant's right,' Nick muttered.

'I'm a superhero.' Alex flexed his biceps. 'And that's my costume.'

'Well, I hope you're invulnerable to pain, Electroman,' Nick smirked. 'Dad's really upset about you cutting up Mum's washing line. Where is it?'

Alex groaned. 'I left it up at Mount Lara.'

As the day wore on, Riana was beginning to give up hope of ever finding Paul. The city was too big and there were too many people.

On the footpath ahead, a teenage girl was kneeling over a piece of canvas. Her clothes were ragged but her dark hair was meticulously braided with shiny beads. Riana moved out of the stream of pedestrians and looked over the girl's shoulder. She was drawing on the canvas with coloured chalk. The drawing showed a muscular woman wielding a sword against a huge creature with scaly wings. The drawing glowed with vibrant reds, greens and purples.

'Like it?' the girl asked.

'Yes,' Riana said. The fearsome beast was very life-like. 'No-one draws like that where I come from. What sort of beast is it?'

'A dragon.'

'I'd love to see one. Where do they live?'

The girl laughed. A man stopped to look at the drawing, then threw some coins into a tin. One missed and rolled along the pavement. Riana picked it up.

'Give that back,' the girl snapped.

'What is it?'

'It's mine, that's what it is.'

The girl held out her hand and Riana gave her the coin.

A thin, scruffy-looking boy hurried over. 'Can I have an icecream now?' he asked.

'No, we need that to buy dinner. Don't ask again.'

As the girl turned back to her drawing, she noticed a man in a blue uniform approaching. 'The fuzz! Let's split.'

She quickly rolled up the canvas and threw her chalks into a bag. The boy grabbed the tin of money and they hurried away, disappearing down an alley.

Riana picked up a piece of chalk the girl had left behind. She knelt and tried it out on the footpath.

The uniformed council officer stopped beside her. 'You kids are obstructing the street. If you don't move on, I'll have to give you a ticket.'

'So I can ride on the train?' Riana asked hopefully.

'Don't get smart with me!' the officer snapped. 'Go home.'

'I can't,' Riana said, struggling not to cry.

The man softened. 'Look, it's not my job to sort out your family problems. The law is the law and you're breaking it.'

Riana got to her feet, staring at the man in fear. In her world, breaking any of the laws brought a terrible punishment from the Spellbinders. 'Are you going to banish me?' she whispered.

The officer laughed. 'Banish you? Oh no, my girl. A by-laws infringement notice is much worse than that.'

Riana backed away from the officer, then turned and ran for her life.

Maran and her children were hidden behind bales of hay in the barn loft. Arla peered through a crack in the wall at the men who were still searching the village.

'What if the Spellbinders found Da?' she asked her mother.

'Your father is safe,' Maran answered. 'I'm sure of it.'

'Ma, I'm hungry,' Jal said. 'How much longer do we have to stay here?'

'It will be dark soon. Then we can go to the forest.'

'How long will we have to stay there?' Arla asked.

'I don't know.'

'Ma,' Jal whispered.

'What now?' Maran said irritably.

Jal pointed. Maran turned to look, and froze with fear. The Spellbinder Ashka was staring down at her.

Hospitality

The morning sunlight shone onto Paul's face. He was lying in his bed, still wearing the clothes from Riana's world. He slowly opened his eyes, closed them, then opened them again. 'I *am* home.'

'Morning.'

Paul looked over the edge of the bed and saw Christine smiling up at him from a mattress on the floor. 'What are you doing down there?'

'Dad let me sleep here. I didn't want you to disappear again.' Christine got up and sat on the bed. 'How are you feeling? Does your head hurt?'

'No.' Paul wondered why Christine was worried about his head. It was his stomach that was injured.

'Do you remember the story you told us

about the Spellbinders?' Christine asked.

'It wasn't a story,' Paul insisted. 'It's the truth.'

'OK,' she said quickly. 'I'm glad you're back.' She snuggled up against Paul, then pulled away. 'You stink! When was the last time you washed?'

'I think it was about a week ago.'

'Ugh! Get out of those clothes and have a shower.'

Grinning, Paul grabbed his sister in a bear hug.

'Let me go, you pig,' she cried and they rolled around the bed, laughing.

Brian's study was like a small laboratory. Benches and shelves were filled with electronic components and testing equipment. Filing cabinets, a desk and a computer took up the rest of the space. Brian was talking angrily into the telephone. 'My son has undergone a harrowing ordeal. He's in no condition to talk to anyone ... No, he wasn't abducted by aliens.'

As he slammed the phone down, Paul and Christine came in. Paul had showered and changed into clean clothes.

'The phone's been ringing since seven,' Brian told them. 'The police told the press you'd been found. Everyone wants to know where you've been.'

'I don't think we should tell anyone about the Spellbinders' land,' Paul said.

'Neither do I,' his father agreed, hiding his disappointment. He'd hoped that after a good night's sleep, Paul would have come to his senses.

The phone rang again and Christine picked it up. 'Hello? No, there's nobody called Paul here. You must have the wrong number.' She grinned as she hung up.

'Dad, can we go and look for Riana?' Paul asked.

'Where would we even start? The police are much better equipped to find her than us. Why don't I get you some breakfast and then you can go back to bed? You still look exhausted. I'll wake you if there's any news.'

Paul nodded and went out with Christine. Brian watched him go, wondering how long it would take his son to get better.

Riana was sleeping under a pile of sacks when she was jolted awake by a loud rumbling. Then she began to bounce up and down. Riana got shakily to her feet and looked around. She was standing in the bucket of a front-end loader which was being driven across a construction site. Riana and the startled driver stared at each other, then he hit the brakes. Riana leaped out of the bucket, ran to the fence and scrambled over it.

As she hurried away, Riana wondered if she would ever find Paul in this dangerous world. She wondered if he was looking for her.

Riana passed the entrance to a park and saw the ragged girl with the braided hair doing another chalk drawing on the footpath. Riana stopped beside her and the girl looked up. 'Are you following me?'

'No. I need your help. I have to find a boy called Paul.'

'I don't know any boys called Paul. Sorry.' She went back to her drawing.

'Please,' Riana begged. 'I don't know anybody here. I don't know what to do.'

'Find a cop. They're supposed to help people.'

'What's a cop?'

'Look, cut the weird act,' the girl said sharply. 'I've got enough problems of my own. Now get lost. You're scaring people away.'

Feeling miserable, Riana went into the park. A sprinkler on the end of a hose sprayed water onto a flower bed. Riana cupped her hands under the spray and drank.

The scruffy young boy she had seen the day before came out of a small brick building. He had his head down, playing with something that made a high-pitched beeping. He was concentrating so hard that he didn't see two teenage toughs who were blocking his path. He collided with them and a rectangular box fell from his hand to the grass.

'Watch where you're going,' one of them said.

'Sorry.' The boy bent to pick up his box but the bigger tough got to it first. 'That's mine,' the boy protested.

'Not anymore.'

The boy tried to snatch the box back but the

toughs tossed it between each other so he couldn't get it.

'Leave him alone,' Riana yelled.

'Who's going to make us?' the big tough sneered.

The boy snatched the box back and ran across the park. The toughs went after him but Riana lifted the hose. They tripped over it and sprawled on the grass.

'You're dead,' the big one said, getting to his feet.

Before they could do anything, the toughs were drenched in a spray of water. They whirled round and saw the girl from the street holding the sprinkler on them.

'Now nick off,' she shouted, 'or I'll scream for the cops!'

The toughs ran off, dripping water.

'Thanks for helping my brother,' the girl said to Riana. 'What's your name?'

'Riana.'

'I'm Josie and this is Ben. I'm sorry I gave you a hard time before. Are you in some kind of trouble?'

'Yes. I'm lost. I don't know what to do.'

'Where are you from?'

'I can't tell you.'

'Where are your parents?'

'I don't know what's happened to them.'

Riana choked back a sob as she thought of her family at Ashka's mercy.

'Can Riana come and stay with us?' Ben asked his sister.

'We were living on this farm up north and there was a flash-flood,' Ben told Riana as they tramped through the city. 'Mum and Dad drowned. Josie looks after me now.'

Josie led the way across a footbridge over a railway line. Ahead was a squat grey building. Sunlight gleamed off its broken windows.

'This is where we live,' Ben said.

Josie went to a boarded-up window in the ground floor of the building. She looked around to make certain no-one was watching, then pulled a piece of board away. Ben climbed through the window and Riana and Josie followed him.

Riana looked around the gloomy space. The low ceiling was supported by rows of thick columns. Paint was peeling off the walls and some of the floorboards were rotting.

'Welcome to our home,' Josie said.

In a corner were two chairs with broken legs, a couple of worn mattresses and a table made of old boards piled on milk crates. Josie had drawn some pictures on the walls and their bright colours made the place seem almost cheerful.

'Hungry?' Josie asked.

Riana nodded. She hadn't eaten since leaving Clayhill the previous day.

'I'll get a fire going and we can have some noodles. Ben, you can chop some onions.'

Josie went to a stack of thick paperback books. She tore some pages from one and began laying a fire in a circle of blackened concrete.

'I'll light it,' Riana said. She squatted by the fireplace and was getting out her flint and steel when Josie held out a small box. Riana opened it. Inside were some short sticks with red ends. To Josie's amazement, Riana scattered the matches over the paper and then used her flint and steel to strike a spark into some sawdust.

She put some paper on the smouldering sawdust and blew on it. The paper and matches burst into flames.

'Neat trick,' Josie said. 'Where'd you learn it?'

'My father taught me.'

'Lucky you. My father didn't teach me anything. He left my mum before I was born.'

'I thought your father drowned,' Riana said.

'No, that was Ben's dad. My mother got married again. We came to the city to look for *my* father. The welfare people wanted to split us up. They were going to put Ben in a home without me.'

'That would never happen in my world,' Riana said.

'What do you mean, "your world"?' Josie asked.

Riana didn't reply.

'Riana, you can trust us,' Josie said. 'We're on our own too. If you don't tell us what's happened, we can't help you.'

'I just need to find Paul,' Riana said.

'Paul who? Don't you know his other name?'

'It's Ren ... something.'

Josie picked up one of the thick books and leafed through the pages. 'Renmark? Rennie? Reynolds?'

'Reynolds.'

'There're hundreds of Reynoldses here,' Josie said, pointing to the columns of names on the pages of the telephone book. 'Do you know Paul's father's name?'

Riana shook her head.

After dinner, Ben showed Riana the box that beeped. He called it a Gameboy and showed her how to play the games inside it.

'Push the jump button,' Ben coached. 'That's it. Now go straight on. Watch out for the mushroom! Go left ... left!'

The box made a squawk and played some tinny music. Riana laughed. 'I got killed by a mushroom.'

Josie finished washing the dinner bowls in a bucket. 'OK, matey, time for your lessons.'

'Can't it wait?' Ben moaned. 'Riana's just getting the hang of this.'

'No.'

Ben reluctantly got a tattered book from his bed.

'I wish Ben could go to school,' Josie said to Riana. 'I can't teach him that much. He barely knows how to read.'

'I can't read at all,' Riana said, to Josie's surprise.

'If *she* can't read, why do I have to learn?' Ben asked.

'I'm not having my brother grow up to be an idiot,' Josie snapped. 'The world's got enough of them as it is. No offence, Riana.'

Ben sat by the fire and opened his book. He started to read. ' " 'How are we going to cross the river?' asked Willy. The kna .. kni ...' "'

'Knight,' Josie prompted.

' "The knight smiled. 'You'll have to use your brian.' " '

'It's brain,' Josie corrected.

'It's "Brian," ' cried Riana. 'Brian's the name of Paul's father!'

Josie grabbed the phone book and flipped through it.

'What is that book?' Riana asked.

'A telephone directory,' Ben said. 'It's got the name of everyone who lives in the city and where they live.'

'Does it have your father's name?'

'We don't know what it is,' Ben said. 'After he left, Mum went back to her old name.'

'Yes!' Josie exclaimed. 'There're only about twenty B. Reynoldses listed. Tomorrow we'll call them all until we find Paul.'

'But the city is huge,' Riana said. 'How will they hear you calling?'

Josie stared at her in disbelief.

'We'll use a telephone,' Ben said.

'What's a telephone?'

'It's ... a thing for talking over long distances.'

'Like an Eyestone.'

'A what?' Josie asked.

Riana realised she had said too much and didn't reply.

'Where are you from?' Josie asked again.

'I ... come from another world,' Riana said hesitantly. 'It's ruled by the Spellbinders. They live in a big castle ...'

'Riana,' Josie said sharply, 'if you don't want to tell us the truth, you don't have to. Just don't treat us like idiots, OK? Ben, keep reading.'

Paul swallowed a mouthful of stodgy microwaved lasagne, wishing his father could cook. Brian pushed his chair back from the dining table and stood up. 'To the Reynolds family! Back together again.' He raised his glass of wine and Paul and Christine joined in the toast with glasses of milk.

'In Clayhill, that's Riana's village,' Paul said, 'we drank milk straight from the cow. It tasted great.'

Christine looked at her father. Was Paul making this up too? Brian decided he'd better clear things up. 'Paul, I know things haven't been ... the best between us since your mother died ... um ... Sometimes people can't say the things they want to ... when they want to ... to the people they want to.'

'What are you trying to say, Dad?' Paul asked, trying not to laugh. His father had never been comfortable talking about things other than science.

'That from now on, things are going to be different. I'm going to be a better listener, a better father. I guess you had time to think things out while you were lost ...'

'I wasn't lost,' Paul protested.

'If you say so,' Brian said calmly. 'I just want you to know that whenever you're ready to talk about what really happened ...'

'I told you what happened,' Paul cut in. 'Don't you believe me?'

'Of course I do. Listen, why don't I call the police and see if they've heard anything about Riana?'

Brian quickly left the room. Paul looked at his sister. 'I'm not making this up.'

Christine didn't know what to think.

The rumble of early morning traffic filtered into the gloomy building. Josie and Ben were asleep on one of the mattresses. Riana was on the other.

'Can you hear me, dear?' a woman's voice asked.

Riana opened her eyes and found herself staring into the concerned face of a Salvation Army officer.

'It's a raid,' Josie yelled, scrambling to her feet. As she pulled Ben up, a male officer came through the door.

'You can't keep living like this,' he said. 'Why don't you come to the shelter with us?'

'You're not splitting us up,' Josie yelled. 'Run!'

Grabbing her bag of chalks, Josie hauled Ben towards the door. Riana went after them but stepped unsuspectingly on some rotting floorboards. They gave way and Riana fell heavily to the floor, crying out as her ankle twisted painfully. The Salvation Army officers hurried to help her.

'It's alright, sweetheart,' the woman said. 'We'll take you to a hospital.'

'St Matthew's is the closest,' the man, suggested.

He looked around for Josie and Ben, but they were gone.

Riana sat nervously in a wheelchair as the Salvation Army officers pushed her towards the hospital entrance. Over the doorway was a caduceus, the doctor's symbol. Riana stared in horror at the two entwined snakes. She grabbed the wheels of the chair, stopping it.

'What's the matter?' the female officer asked.

'That's the Spellbinders' sign,' Riana said fearfully. 'Paul said there were no Spellbinders in this world.'

'Don't be frightened,' the woman said gently, 'that's just the sign for a hospital.'

The man gently removed Riana's hands from the wheels and pushed her through the entrance.

Though it was early in the morning, the casualty department of St Matthew's Hospital was already busy. Riana was awed by the bright lights, strange smells and constant stream of patients that passed as she waited to be seen. Eventually a young doctor arrived and began to examine her swollen ankle. Riana looked up and stared as a girl dressed in black leather with purple spiked hair and rings in her nose walked past. The girl went over to a wall and pressed a button. A section of the wall slid aside, revealing a small room. The girl went in and the wall closed.

'How many fingers am I holding up?' the doctor asked.

Riana looked at his hand. 'Three.'

The doctor pointed to the wall. 'What time does the clock say?'

'What's a clock?' Riana asked.

The wall opened again and Riana was shocked to see an old woman come out. 'What happened to the girl?'

The doctor just looked at her.

'A girl went through that wall,' Riana explained. 'When she came out, she was old.'

The doctor laughed. 'Let's go and get that ankle X-rayed.' He started to wheel Riana towards the lift.

'No,' Riana cried. 'I don't want to go in there. I don't want to get old!'

She leaped out of the wheelchair, crying out as she put weight on her injured ankle. The doctor tried to grab her but Riana dodged around a trolley and hobbled towards the exit.

'Stop her,' the doctor yelled.

An orderly grabbed Riana just as she reached the doors.

'Call the psychiatric registrar,' the doctor called to a nurse. 'Tell her I'm bringing a patient up.' He beckoned to the orderly, who carried Riana towards the lift.

'Let me go,' Riana cried, struggling in his arms. 'No!'

The lift doors closed, blocking out Riana's cries.

Paul nervously approached his school, hoping he could slip quietly in and find Alex and Katrina without being noticed.

'It's Paul,' Katrina's friend Lisa screeched.

In seconds, Paul was surrounded by excited students, bombarding him with questions about his disappearance.

'Leave him alone,' Alex yelled, elbowing through the crowd. 'He's had a rough time. Go!'

The students slowly dispersed.

'Thanks, mate,' Paul said. Alex suddenly hid behind him. 'What are you doing?'

'I don't want Katrina's mum to see me.'

Paul followed Alex's gaze and saw Katrina getting out of her mother's car.

'I expect to see you here at 3.30 sharp,' Mrs Muggleton called as she drove away.

Katrina entered the schoolyard and went

over to Paul and Alex. She looked furious.

'What's up?' Alex asked.

'I've been totally grounded. Mum and Dad think you're my boyfriend.'

Alex gave an embarrassed laugh.

'What happened with the police?' Katrina asked Paul. 'Where's Riana?'

'I don't know. I came to see if you guys would help me look for her.'

The school bell sounded. Alex clutched his stomach and groaned. 'All of a sudden, I don't feel so well. I think I'd better have the day off. How are you feeling, Katrina?'

'If I get caught wagging school, Dad won't just ground me, he'll bury me. Sorry.'

She headed for class. Paul and Alex hurried out of the school.

Riana hobbled across the hospital consulting room, her ankle strapped in a white bandage. She tried to open the door but it was locked. She limped to the window and looked out. It was a long way to the ground. Behind her, the door opened and a woman in a white coat came in.

'Sorry to keep you waiting, Riana,' she said. 'I'm Dr Lim.'

Riana stared at her face. 'What happened to your eyes?'

'I'm Chinese. Haven't you ever seen a Chinese person before?'

Riana shook her head.

'Don't you watch TV or look at newspapers?'

Riana shook her head again.

'Where do you live, Riana?'

Riana didn't answer.

'Riana, I'm a psychiatrist. Whatever you say is just between you and me. Do your parents know where you are?'

Riana started to cry.

Jal was on the floor of the cottage, playing with Correon's magic stones. Maran sat despondently by the window. Ashka had made her a prisoner in her own home, and two village men she had known her whole life were standing guard outside the door. Arla came over and stood by her mother. 'Will Riana ever come home?'

'Of course she will,' Maran answered. 'She's probably just having a lot of fun in Paul's world.'

Through the window, Arla saw Ashka, Gryvon and the Summoner approaching. 'What's going to happen to us?' Arla asked.

Before Maran could answer, there was a loud knocking on the door.

'Come out, Maran,' Ashka called, 'and bring your children.'

'Don't let the Spellbinder see that you are frightened,' Maran told Jal. She took his hand and led him to the door. Arla picked up the magic stones and followed them.

The whole village watched as Maran and her children came out of the cottage and stood before Ashka.

'Your husband is an enemy of the Spellbinders,' Ashka declared.

'He's a good man,' Maran protested.

'Tell me where he is!'

Maran said nothing.

'If you don't tell me, I'll burn your cottage.'

Anger flashed in Maran's eyes. 'I don't know where he is! And I wouldn't tell you if I did.'

Ashka energised her power suit and hurled a bolt of energy at the thatched roof of the cottage. The dry grass burst into flames.

'This whole village shows disrespect to the Spellbinders,' Ashka shouted. 'If Bron is not caught within the week, all of Clayhill will be burnt to the ground.'

'Spellbinder, please ...' the Summoner spluttered.

'Lock them up,' Ashka ordered.

The terrified Summoner pushed Maran and her children towards the storehouse in the middle of the square. Maran cast a tearful look back at her burning home.

'It's alright, Ma,' Arla whispered. 'I saved Correon's magic stones. They'll keep us safe.'

Maran tried to smile, but her lips barely moved.

The front door of Paul's house banged open and Paul and Alex trudged in. They looked

51

tired. Their search for Riana had been useless.

'Face it, mate,' Alex said. 'We've got as much chance of finding Riana as the Eskimos have of winning the World Cup.'

Paul nodded despondently, then noticed the blinking light on the answering machine by the telephone.

'Maybe the police have found her.' He pushed the replay button.

'Hi,' a girl's voice said. 'My name is Josie. I've got a message for a Paul Reynolds. If you're a friend of Riana's, she needs your help. She was taken to St Matthew's Hospital this morning.'

There was a beep as the message ended.

'I've got to get Dad to take me there,' Paul said excitedly. 'Once he meets Riana, he'll have to believe me.'

Brian sat in his office in the Magnetronix building. He was the chief scientist of the company, which specialised in the research and development of electronic technology. The owner, a ball of energy on legs named Eric, was pacing around Brian's office.

'And if we get this contract,' Eric said, 'it'll open up the whole Asian market. Now that you're back, I want you on it. One hundred and ten per cent.'

'You don't have to worry, Eric. Now that Paul's been found, I'm here full-time. There'll be no more interruptions.'

The door opened and Paul burst in. 'Dad, I've found Riana. She's in St Matthew's Hospital. We've got to get her out: she doesn't know this world; she'll be scared out of her mind.'

'What's going on, Brian?' Eric asked anxiously.

'Paul's still a little ... disturbed by his recent experience,' Brian said awkwardly. He hurried Paul out of the office and into the corridor. 'Go home and go back to bed. I'll be there as soon as I can.'

'But, Dad,' Paul protested.

'I'm going to call a taxi. When I get back we'll talk about all this.'

Paul watched sadly as Brian went back into his office.

'You've got a visitor, Riana.'

Riana sat up in bed. The nurse beckoned and Paul came in. Riana leaped out of the bed and flung her arms around him.

'What did you tell them?' Paul asked Riana after the nurse had gone.

'Nothing.'

'Put your clothes on and let's go.'

'Hello.' Paul turned and saw a doctor coming through the door. 'I'm Dr Lim. I understand you're a friend of Riana's.'

Paul noticed the badge on the doctor's jacket. It read 'Psychiatric Unit'.

'Riana doesn't need a psychiatrist,' Paul said. 'She's not crazy.'

'No-one's saying she is. What's your name?'

'Paul ... Paul Correon. Riana, let's go.'

Dr Lim moved in front of the door. 'I'm sorry but Riana is legally under age. I can't release her without permission from her parents.'

'But her parents are in ...' Paul stopped.

'Where, Paul?'

Paul realised he'd better shut up. 'Don't worry, Riana, I'll get you out of here.' He pushed past the doctor and went out.

Riana tried to go after him but the doctor blocked her way.

Gasping for breath, Bron stumbled out of the forest. Ahead was a steep, rocky cliff. Though his legs were aching, Bron staggered towards it. He was still clutching the bag containing Paul's video-camera.

Gryvon and two of the men from the village emerged from the trees and started to run after him. Bron reached the cliff but he was too weak to climb. He scrambled into the rocks at its base and huddled behind a large outcrop. He heard the shouts of the search party approaching.

Suddenly, a hand clamped over Bron's mouth and he was dragged through a narrow fissure into a cave.

As Bron struggled to get free, he heard a familiar voice: 'Let him go, Zander.'

Bron was released. He peered through the gloom and saw that his captor was a young man. Further back in the cave stood Correon, the old, white-haired Spellbinder. Bron dropped to his knees. 'Spellbinder, help me!'

'I'm not a Spellbinder anymore.' Correon helped Bron up. 'Do you know what happened to Paul?'

'Paul's gone back to his world. He took Riana with him. I don't know how to get her back.'

'They're starting to search the rocks,' Zander called in a low voice from the cave entrance. 'We'll have to run.'

'I can't,' Bron said. 'My legs won't take it.'

'Give me your coat and hat.'

Zander quickly put on Bron's clothes and slipped out of the cave.

'There he is,' came a shout from outside. The sounds of pursuit moved away.

Bron slumped gratefully against the cave wall and closed his eyes.

'My dad thinks I'm crazy,' Paul said as Alex closed the garage door. 'And the shrink thinks Riana's crazy.'

Alex went to a corner of the garage and lifted the old blanket. The power suit was underneath.

'If I get this working,' Paul said, 'Dad will have to believe me.' He put the power suit on the bench.

'You said the suit was dead,' Alex pointed out.

'The powerstones can be recharged.' Paul opened the housings on the belt and carefully lifted out the two dull stones. 'The Spellbinders did it with a huge electro-magnet in their castle.'

'At the docks they use big electro-magnets to lift containers onto ships.'

'Alex, you can't just walk onto the docks and say "Hey, let me recharge my powerstones".'

'Dummy! Don't you remember where my father works?'

Paul grinned. 'Katsonis, you're a genius.'

Alex nodded. 'I've always thought so.'

The security guard escorted Paul and Alex through the Glebe Island container terminal to the base of a huge crane. Paul promised not to move while the man accompanied Alex up the ladder to his father. As soon as they were out of sight, Paul pulled the power suit and powerstones from his bag.

Mr Katsonis was sitting in the cab of the crane high above the terminal. Under his careful control, the crane lowered a cargo container into the hold of a ship. He pulled a lever and the electro-magnets released the container and lifted away. Alex's head appeared in the doorway.

'Alex, what are you doing here?'

'I've come to visit my favourite father,' Alex said innocently, climbing into the cramped space as the security guard waited on the ladder.

'If you're after money,' said Mr Katsonis, 'the answer's no.'

Below the crane, Paul realised that no-one could see him. He finished tying the powerstones together with cord and then hurried over to a container as the electro-magnets descended towards it. He tossed the powerstones and they landed on top of the

58

container. Energy crackled around them as the magnets approached.

In the crane cab, Mr Katsonis pulled a lever and the crane began lifting the heavy container off the dock.

'Pop, wait,' Alex shouted, 'there's something near the container! It could be a person.'

Stavros pushed the lever and the container was lowered. As the magnets disconnected, Paul yanked on the cord. The powerstones flew off the container and he caught them. The stones were now gleaming with energy. Paul hurried away just as Alex, his father and the security guard climbed down the ladder from the crane. They looked around.

'There's nothing there,' the guard said.

Alex shrugged innocently. 'I guess I was wrong.'

'Dinner time, Riana,' the nurse said cheerily as she came into Riana's room with a tray. The bed was empty. The nurse rushed out to find Dr Lim.

At the end of the corridor, an orderly wheeled a trolley into a linen room. He began pulling dirty sheets from the trolley and tossing them down a chute that led to the laundry.

'Bob,' Dr Lim called from the doorway, 'keep a look out, will you? One of the patients is loose. Teenage girl.'

'Don't worry, Doc,' the orderly said. 'The only way out of here is down this chute. And to get down there, she's got to get past me.' He flexed his biceps and struck a strongman pose. The doctor laughed and went out.

The orderly pulled another sheet from the trolley. Riana was beneath it. She pushed the surprised orderly away and made a dive for the chute. The orderly grabbed her legs and pulled her back out.

'Let me go,' Riana sobbed, 'I want to go home!'

The sun had just gone down as Alex searched between the containers in the terminal. 'Paul?' he called softly.

Alex yelped as Paul stepped out of the darkness. He was wearing the Spellbinder power suit. In the glow of an overhead light, he looked like an alien warrior out of a science fiction movie.

'Did it work?' Alex asked.

'Let's find out.' Paul struck his wrists together and a spark flew between them. Energy crackled over the copper studs on the power suit and Paul grinned.

Suddenly, electricity began sparking around the power lines overhead. As Paul and Alex looked up, the light above them exploded. The boys dived to the ground. Around them, other lights started going out and the terminal was plunged into darkness.

Alex stared at Paul in horror. 'What have you done?'

Breakout

'Do something,' Alex yelled at Paul. Cries of alarm were coming from all around the container terminal. 'Turn it off!' He ducked flying glass as another overhead light shattered.

Paul opened the housings on the power suit belt and pulled out the powerstones. Energy stopped crackling around the power lines and lights started coming back on.

'What happened?' Alex asked.

'The power suit's electro-magnetic field must have disrupted the electricity supply.' Paul grinned at Alex. 'When Dad sees this, he'll have to believe me.'

'If my dad sees us, we're toast. Let's go.'

'Dad! Dad!' Paul shouted as he and Alex burst through the front door. They ran into the kitchen and stopped. Christine and an athletic, dark-haired young woman were dancing to a song playing on the radio.

'Hi, Paul,' Christine said. 'This is Gina. Dad's hired her to look after us while he's at work. She's great.'

Gina twirled Christine around a final time then switched the radio off. 'Mr Reynolds told me about you being lost,' she said to Paul. 'It must have been awful.' She smiled and Alex immediately fell in love with her.

'Where is Dad?' Paul asked.

'He's working overnight at the lab. I'd better call him and let him know you're OK. He was worried.'

Gina started towards the door. Paul got there first. 'I'll do it.' He ran out.

Alex smiled at Gina. 'Hi, I'm Alex. What's for dinner? I always eat here on Tuesdays.'

'Dad, I've got to show you something,' Paul said excitedly into the telephone in the hall. 'When will you be home?'

'Hopefully, I'll see you for breakfast,' Brian replied. 'Did you meet Gina?'

'Yes.'

'Please don't give her a hard time. Listen, I'm sorry about this afternoon.'

Paul heard an alarm go off in his father's laboratory.

'Shut it down,' Brian yelled. 'Sorry, Paul, things are a bit frantic here at the moment. Have a good sleep. We'll talk in the morning.'

The phone went dead. Paul slammed the receiver down.

Alex came out of the kitchen eating a bowl of spaghetti. 'You've lucked out, mate. Not only is Gina a spunk, she makes a great spaghetti.'

'Forget that,' Paul snapped. 'We've got to get Riana out of the hospital.'

'There's nothing we can do now. We'll go and see her at lunchtime tomorrow.'

'Paul,' Gina called from the kitchen, 'come and get your dinner.'

'Just what I don't need,' Paul groaned. 'A babysitter.'

'I'd be a baby if Gina was looking after me,' Alex said lecherously. Paul punched him.

Bron squatted by a fire in the cave, gulping stew straight from the pot. Beside him, Correon was staring at the screen on the back of Paul's video-camera. He was watching the tape Paul had secretly made of Ashka in the Spellbinders' castle.

'You want the gunpowder to use against the Regents,' Paul's voice said off-screen. 'You want to rule the Spellbinders.'

On the screen, Ashka smiled. 'Very perceptive. And when I do, I can make your life here very pleasant. Or very unpleasant.'

Correon switched off the tape and turned to Bron. 'This is wonderful. When the Regents see it, Ashka is finished as a Spellbinder.'

'What about Riana? Will the Regents help me get her back from Paul's world?'

'One thing at a time, Bron.'

A sound came from outside the cave and Correon and Bron leaped up in alarm. Zander came in breathing heavily.

'I thought Gryvon had caught you,' Correon said.

Zander grinned. 'I led them round in circles. They're totally confused.' He threw off Bron's coat and hat, went to the fire and scooped up some stew.

'Eat quickly,' Correon said. 'We're going to the Spellbinders' castle.'

Zander looked warily out of the cave. There was no sign of the search party. He emerged into the sunlight with Correon. Bron followed, carrying the bag with the video-camera. Zander and Correon started walking. Bron went in the opposite direction.

'Bron, the castle is this way,' Zander called.

'I left my family in Clayhill. I'm not going anywhere till I'm sure they're safe.'

He kept walking. Correon scowled.

'It's not that far out of our way,' Zander said.

The old Spellbinder sighed. 'Wait, Bron. We're coming.'

Paul led Alex and Katrina into Riana's hospital room. There was no sign of her and the bed had not been slept in. Paul stormed out in search of Dr Lim.

He found her at the nurses' station outside the psychiatric ward. She and a nurse were watching a bank of video screens which monitored the rooms inside the locked ward.

'Where's Riana?' Paul demanded.

'Riana tried to run away last night,' the doctor explained. 'We had to move her to this security ward. She's refusing to talk.'

'Can I see her?' Paul begged. 'Maybe she'll talk to me.'

'I'm just about to go to my clinic.'

'Please?'

Dr Lim took out a keycard and swiped it through the electronic lock on the door of the ward. There was a loud click as the lock opened.

'Your friends will have to stay out here,' the doctor said.

Paul looked apologetically at Alex and Katrina, then followed the doctor through the door.

Riana anxiously paced the small white hospital room. The door was locked and the window was barred. It was like being back in the Spellbinders' castle. Hearing the lock open, she turned and saw Dr Lim come in with Paul. Riana ran to Paul and hugged him. 'I'm scared,' she whispered. 'Get me out of this place.'

Paul turned to the doctor. 'If I can get my dad to agree, can Riana come home with us?'

Lim shut the door. 'I'm sorry. We can't release Riana until we find her parents.'

'But they're not in this world,' Riana protested.

'What do you mean?' the doctor asked.

Riana hesitated.

'Riana, I can't help if you won't talk to me.'

'We'll have to tell her the truth,' Riana told Paul.

'She'll never believe us.'

'You can trust me,' the doctor said.

Riana hesitated a moment longer, then took the plunge. 'You can't talk to my parents because ... I come from another world. It's called the Spellbinders' land.'

'Riana can't get back there until we find a way to open the energy doorway,' Paul added.

'Paul,' the doctor said firmly, 'I think that's enough for today.'

She opened the door. Paul didn't move. 'I'm

not leaving without Riana,' he said defiantly.

'I don't want to call an orderly ...' the doctor threatened.

Paul realised it was hopeless and turned to go.

'Paul, don't leave me,' Riana cried.

Paul paused at the doorway. 'I'll get you out, Riana. I promise.'

'Maybe we could break Riana out,' Paul suggested as he walked away from the hospital with Alex and Katrina.

'You can't be serious,' Katrina said.

'I owe Riana my life. I have to rescue her.'

'The only way we'd get past the video surveillance is if there was a blackout,' Alex said.

Alex and Paul stopped and looked at each other.

'Are you thinking what I'm thinking?' Paul asked.

Alex grinned.

'The power suit!'

Gryvon stood guard over Riana's family as they stared sadly at the remains of their burnt cottage. Jal was sniffling.

'Don't worry, Jal,' Arla said bravely, 'when Da gets back, we'll build a better house.'

'That's right,' Maran said. 'With a loft just for you.'

Jal smiled at the thought. He stopped when he saw Ashka coming out of the Summoner's cottage.

The Summoner brought her a horse. 'I have posted guards all around the village, Spellbinder. If Bron returns, we'll get him.'

'For the sake of your village, I hope you're right.'

The shaken Summoner bowed. Ashka mounted the horse and started to ride out of the village.

'We have to warn Da,' Arla whispered to Maran.

'Get moving,' Gryvon snapped and gave Maran a shove.

Maran glared at him, then took her children's hands. 'Come on. We're going to see the Spellbinder's castle,' she said cheerily.

'Won't that be exciting?'

Tall trees and thick undergrowth bordered the narrow trail away from Clayhill. Maran, Arla and Jal trudged behind Ashka's horse, breathing its dust. Gryvon brought up the rear.

'I'll hide in the forest and wait for Da,' Arla said quietly to her mother. 'No-one will find me. I can trap a rabbit and I know which mushrooms are safe to eat.'

Maran shook her head. 'It's too dangerous.'

'You'd let Riana do it.'

Maran said nothing. Suddenly, Arla pointed into the trees and screamed. 'Marauders!'

As Gryvon and Ashka turned to look, Arla dived into the thick undergrowth, on the other side of the trail.

'Arla,' Maran cried.

Gryvon started to go after her but Maran blocked his path. Gryvon pushed her aside but Arla had disappeared.

'Leave her,' Ashka said. 'She won't last long in this forest on her own. Two hostages are enough.'

Gryvon pushed Maran and Jal along the trail.

Paul sat on his bed, carefully removing one of the powerstones from the power suit. There was a knock on the door. Paul quickly threw one of his father's lab coats over the power suit lying on the bed.

'What do you want?' Paul asked as Christine came in.

'I want to know what you think of Gina.'

'I guess she's OK. Why?'

'She isn't married. I asked her. What are you doing with that?'

Christine reached for the lab coat on the bed but Paul grabbed her hand. 'I'm borrowing it for school. We're dissecting rats tomorrow in science. Lots of blood and slime and guts.'

Christine pulled a face. She went towards the door and then stopped. 'Gina's a great cook, isn't she?'

'Christine, what are you on about?'

'I'm just thinking.'

'Well, think somewhere else,' Paul snapped. 'I've got homework.'

Christine left in a huff. Paul waited until he heard her bedroom door slam, then wrapped the power suit in the lab coat and hurried out.

Hidden in a clump of bushes, Paul impatiently watched the side-door of the hospital. Alex had been inside for nearly ten minutes. Paul tightened one of the straps on the power suit he was wearing. Tonight, he would find out just what it could do. To his relief, the door opened and Alex came out. He was wearing the lab coat and wheeling a stretcher.

'Any problems?' Paul asked.

'Nah. You can do anything in that place if you're wearing a white coat.' Alex pulled a bandage from his coat pocket and started wrapping it around Paul's head. 'There's an awful lot of electrical equipment in there. I hope the suit doesn't short out the whole hospital.'

'I took out one of the powerstones,' Paul told him. 'That should localise the effect.'

Alex finished the bandage.

'Last chance to back out,' Paul told him.

'Shut up. You're supposed to be concussed.'

Paul grinned. He climbed onto the stretcher and lay back. Alex covered him with a sheet then wheeled him towards the hospital entrance.

No-one gave them a second look as Alex wheeled Paul through the hospital. On the fifth floor, Alex pushed Paul out of the lift and down the deserted corridor towards the security ward.

Paul climbed off the stretcher and he and Alex crept to the corner. They peeked around it. A nurse was at the desk outside the ward.

Alex checked his watch. 'It's 5.59,' he whispered. 'Come on, Katrina.'

At exactly six o'clock, the phone at the nurses' station rang. The nurse picked it up. 'Hello. Psychiatric ward.'

Katrina answered. 'Hi, I'm Dr Lim's daughter. Mum thinks she left her bag in her office. Could you check and see if it's there?'

'Hang on,' the nurse replied. 'I'll go and see.'

Paul and Alex smiled at each other as the nurse picked up a set of keys and disappeared down the corridor. They hurried to the security ward door. Paul struck his wrists together, energising the power suit. A glowing ball of energy formed in his hand.

In her room, Riana put the metal cover back over her unfinished dinner. How could anyone get better when hospital food tasted so awful? Suddenly, the ceiling lights flickered on and off and an alarm bell started ringing. Riana got out of bed and went to the door. It was unlocked. She ran to the wardrobe, pulled out her Clayhill clothes and started to change.

Paul threw the ball of energy. The power-bolt struck the alarm on the wall and Alex gaped as it exploded in a shower of sparks. Paul turned the handle of the ward door. To his relief, the electronic lock had shorted out and the door opened.

'Hey,' the nurse shouted from down the corridor. She started running towards them.

Paul and Alex ran into the security ward. Alex pushed the door shut. 'It won't lock,' he yelled.

Paul fired a power-bolt at the door lock. It melted, jamming the door closed. Paul and Alex ran up the corridor.

Wearing her Clayhill clothes, Riana peered out of her room. The lights in the corridor were flickering. As she started to creep along the corridor, a figure wearing a Spellbinder power suit appeared. Riana ducked back into her room.

As Paul ran into Riana's room, she stepped from behind the door and hurled the metal dish cover which she had filled with water. Sparks flew from the power suit. Riana ran to the door but collided with Alex as he came in. She stared in surprise at Alex, then looked at the dripping Paul. 'I'm sorry,' she wailed, 'I didn't know it was you.'

From the corridor came the sound of splintering wood. Alex ran out of the room and looked around the corner. An axe blade split the wood around the melted lock and the door sprang open. The nurse and two orderlies ran through and started checking the rooms along the corridor.

Alex ran back into Riana's room and closed the door. Paul was drying the powerstone with a bed sheet. 'They'll be here in a sec,' Alex warned. 'Any luck?'

Paul replaced the powerstone in the suit and struck his wrists together. There was no spark. 'It's useless,' Paul said. 'The water shorted out the powerstone.'

'Maybe we could pretend to be crazy too,' Alex suggested. 'They can't put you in gaol if you're crazy.'

'We're not giving up,' Paul said stubbornly.

The nurse and orderlies worked their way up the corridor, checking the rooms.

'Some strange people came into my room,' Riana called from her doorway. 'They went up there.' She pointed to the far end of the corridor.

'Good girl,' the nurse said. 'Go back inside and close the door.'

Riana did as she was told and the nurse and orderlies hurried away. The door to Riana's room opened again and Paul, Riana and Alex crept out. They made their way towards the exit but the nurse turned and saw them. 'There they are,' she shouted.

Paul, Riana and Alex raced out of the security ward and ran for the lifts. Paul hit the button on the wall but the lift doors stayed closed. Alex pointed to the stairwell. 'Down there!'

They started down the stairs as their pursuers ran out of the ward. One orderly ran to the lifts while the other followed the nurse down the stairs.

Paul, Riana and Alex burst out of the stairwell and ran along a corridor. Ahead of them, the lift doors opened. The orderly stepped out and blocked their way. Paul grabbed a laundry trolley and rammed the orderly back into the lift.

'Now what?' Alex asked.

'This way!' Riana ran along the corridor to the linen room and threw the door open. Paul and Alex followed her inside. Riana started pulling on a tall cupboard opposite the door. 'Help me!'

Paul and Alex helped Riana pull the cupboard over. It fell against the door, jamming it shut. Outside, someone started pounding on the door. 'Open up,' the nurse shouted, 'or I'll call the police.'

Alex looked around the room. There was no other exit. 'Good thinking, Riana,' he said sarcastically. 'Now we're trapped here until the cops arrive.'

'No we're not.'

Riana opened the flap of the laundry chute. Paul and Alex looked into its black depths.

'What if it leads to a furnace?' Alex asked.

'Don't be an idiot,' Paul said. 'Why would they burn their sheets?'

'Let's think about this,' Alex said.

There was more pounding on the door.

'You can stay and think,' Riana said. 'I'm going.' She pushed Alex aside, climbed into the chute and slid out of sight.

Riana flew out of the chute and dropped into a laundry hamper in the hospital loading bay. A moment later, Paul landed beside her.

'What about Alex?' Riana asked as she scrambled out of the hamper.

Screaming at the top of his voice, Alex flew out of the chute and landed on Paul. 'I don't believe I did that,' he said with a grin of relief.

'Get off me,' Paul yelled.

It was dark by the time they reached the street where Paul lived. Alex had been babbling about their adventure all the way.

'And did you see the look on that nurse's face when she saw the power suit?' he chortled. 'I bet she thought they'd been invaded by aliens.'

They stopped outside Paul's house. 'Dad's car's not here,' Paul said. 'He must still be at the lab.'

Through the front window they could see Gina watching television in the loungeroom.

'We'll have to sneak in the back way,' Paul told Riana.

'Thank you for rescuing me,' Riana said. 'Both of you.'

'In our world,' Alex said, 'when a boy saves a girl, she gives him a big kiss.' He moved closer to Riana and puckered his lips.

Paul gave him a shove. 'See you in the morning, Alex.'

'Spoilsport,' Alex grumbled and walked away.

Paul and Riana crept into the bedroom, and, with a sigh of relief, Paul closed the door. 'We're safe now.'

Riana looked around the room. It was almost as big as her cottage in Clayhill. 'Is this all yours?' she asked in amazement.

Paul nodded. He opened his wardrobe and hung the power suit inside. On the dresser, Riana noticed a photograph of a woman with her arm around a younger Paul. They were both smiling. 'Who's this?' she asked.

'My mother. It was taken just before she died.'

Riana looked at the picture and thought of her own mother. She let out a tiny sob.

'It's OK, Riana,' Paul said gently. 'I'm sure Maran and Bron are alright. And my dad will find a way to get you home. I promise.'

Bron, Zander and Correon crouched in the trees above Clayhill. Below them, the village looked peaceful. There was no sign of Ashka.

'It looks safe enough,' Bron said. Zander and Correon followed him down the wooded slope.

'Da!'

Bron whirled round and saw Arla step out from behind a fallen tree. She ran to her father, who caught her in a hug. 'What are you doing out here?'

'You have to hide. The Summoner is looking for you.'

'Where are your mother and Jal?'

'The Spellbinder Ashka took them to the castle. She burned our house.'

Bron was furious. Before the others could react, he ran down the hill and plunged through a wheat field to the edge of the village. He stared in dismay at the burnt remains of the home he had built with his own hands. Correon, Zander and Arla hurried up to him. The old Spellbinder put his hand on Bron's shoulder. 'Ashka will pay for this.'

A man came out of the barn and looked their way. 'There's Bron,' he shouted. 'Call the Summoner!'

Bron grabbed Arla's hand and fled with Correon and Zander back into the forest.

Christine watched eagerly as Gina served Brian another slice of French toast. 'Good, isn't it, Dad?'

'It's very nice,' Brian replied through a mouthful.

'Gina's a great cook, isn't she?'

'I like to cook,' Gina said.

'And Dad likes to eat. Isn't that a coincidence?' Christine smiled. Her campaign to get her father and Gina together was going well.

Paul came into the kitchen, dressed for school. Gina handed him a plate.

'Just think, Paul,' Christine said, 'French toast for breakfast every morning.'

Paul stared at Christine, wondering what she was on about.

'Time I was going,' Gina said. 'See you later.'

'We really like having you here, Gina,' Christine said enthusiastically as Gina got her bag. 'Don't we, Dad?'

'Er ... yeah,' said a confused Brian.

Christine saw Gina out.

'I'm sorry for being short with you on the phone yesterday,' Brian said to Paul. 'Work's a bit of a nightmare. What did you want to talk about?'

Paul knew he had to careful about how he explained Riana's presence in his bedroom. He took a deep breath. 'Dad, you know I've been saying some pretty strange things lately ...'

He was interrupted by the raucous sound of a morning cartoon show from the TV in the next room.

'Christine, I don't want you watching that stuff in the mornings,' Brian yelled. 'Turn on the news.'

Christine changed channels and a reporter's voice came from the TV. 'Damage to computers and security equipment at St Matthew's Hospital could run into thousands of dollars.'

Paul leaped to his feet and raced out of the kitchen. Christine was curled up on the sofa in front of the TV. On the screen was a shot of the reporter standing outside St Matthew's hospital. 'Doctors say it was a miracle no patients were injured,' the reporter continued. 'Police wish to interview a boy called Paul Correon ...'

Paul grabbed the remote control and switched the TV off. Brian appeared at the kitchen door. 'I thought you wanted to talk to me?'

Paul's mind raced. How could he tell his father that he'd wrecked a hospital? Suddenly, rap music blared from upstairs. Brian's eyes shot suspiciously towards the ceiling.

'I ... left a tape running,' Paul said quickly. 'I'd better turn it off.' He ran up the stairs.

The music in Paul's bedroom was deafening. Riana was desperately pushing buttons on the mini hi-fi, trying to turn it off. Paul ran in and pulled the plug out of the wall socket.

'I'm sorry,' Riana said. 'Is your father ready to meet me now?'

Paul slumped on the bed. 'I couldn't tell him. We did a lot of damage at the hospital last night.'

'But your father was going to help me get home.'

'Paul, come on,' Brian called, 'I'll drop you at school.'

'We'll sort everything out when I get back,' Paul promised. 'Make yourself at home. Wear some of my clothes.' He grabbed his school bag and headed for the door.

'Paul, I'm hungry,' Riana said.

'Wait until everyone's gone then help yourself from the fridge.' Paul went out, shutting the door.

A moment later, he came back in. 'It's the big white box in the kitchen.' He ran out, closed the door, then raced straight back in again. 'And stay inside. Don't let anyone see you.'

Paul raced out again, leaving Riana totally bewildered.

Paul stood at the school gate and waved as his father drove away. He turned around to find Alex and Katrina standing behind him. Katrina held up a newspaper. The headline read, 'YOUTHS WRECK HOSPITAL.' 'You were supposed to break Riana out, not destroy the hospital,' she said angrily.

'Things got a bit out of hand,' Paul admitted.

'Out of hand?' Katrina yelled. 'We could go to gaol!'

'No we won't. The police can't trace us. No-one knows who we are.'

'Did you tell your Dad about Riana?' Alex asked.

'I didn't dare.'

'So where is she?'

'At home.'

'On her own?' Katrina asked incredulously.

Riana crept down the stairs and looked around. She wondered which of the many rooms was the kitchen. Then she noticed a white box, taller than her, standing against a wall. She guessed it must be the fridge Paul had mentioned. This must be the kitchen, but there was no food to be seen and nowhere to light a fire.

Riana went over to the fridge and pulled on the handle. The freezer door opened and frosty air spilled out. Riana wondered what made it so cold. She pulled out a large icecream container and opened it. She poked at the hard white substance inside but couldn't work out what it was for. She replaced the lid and put it back in the freezer, upside down.

Leaving the freezer door ajar, Riana opened the bottom door of the fridge and smiled: here was food that she recognised. She took out onions, potatoes and a piece of steak and looked around for somewhere to cook them.

A short while later, a small wood fire was burning on top of the electric stove, filling the room with smoke. Riana used a meat cleaver to hack off another piece of the tree branch she had pulled though the window. She added the wood to the fire, then used the cleaver to stir the steak and vegetables which were sizzling in a wok over the flames. Behind her, the doors of the refrigerator were still open. Melted icecream and water were starting to drip onto the floor.

By the time school was over, Paul was exhausted. He had spent most of the day worrying that he would be called out of class to talk to the police about last night. As he approached his house, he heard loud music. Christine wouldn't be home yet, so it must be Riana. He started to run.

Paul burst into the loungeroom and stared. On the TV, a muscular aerobics instructor was demonstrating exercises to music. Riana lay on the floor, following the routine.

'Join in, Paul,' she yelled over the music. 'Carl says everyone should be doing this.'

Paul turned the TV off. 'Not now. We have to hide you before Christine gets home.'

As he headed towards the stairs, Paul looked into the kitchen. It was a disaster area. The wall above the stove was blackened from the cooking fire. Melted icecream and water had pooled on the floor in front of the fridge. As Paul stared in horror at the damage, the back door opened and Christine came in.

'I had an accident,' Paul said quickly. 'But I'll clean it up. Why don't you go out and play?' He went to push Christine out the door but slipped in the icecream and crashed to the floor.

Riana ran in. 'Paul, are you alright?'

'Who are you?' Christine asked.

Lying in a pool of liquid icecream, Paul groaned in dismay.

The Trojan Toffee Trolley

Paul got up from the kitchen floor, wiping melted icecream from his clothes. 'Christine, this is Riana,' he said nervously.

'The girl from the Spellbinder world?' Christine asked, staring at Riana in astonishment. Paul nodded.

'I knew you weren't crazy,' Christine said. 'Where did you find her?'

'Well ...' Paul began.

'Paul rescued me from the hospital last night,' Riana said.

Christine stared admiringly at her brother. 'That was you on the news? Wow! You're in a lot of trouble.'

'I will be if anyone finds out,' Paul told her. 'We have to keep Riana a secret. Especially from Dad. You have to promise.'

Christine smiled. 'I will, if you help me get

Dad and Gina together.'

'Dad and Gina?'

'Yeah. Wouldn't Gina make a great mum?'

'You're out of your skull!'

'Dad, do you know where Paul was last night?' Christine asked in a little girl voice.

Paul knew when he was beaten. 'Alright! It's a deal.'

Riana laughed. 'Christine, you're just like my sister.'

Christine smiled. 'Paul said you helped him escape from the Spellbinders' castle. What was it like? Were you frightened?'

Before Riana could answer, they heard the front door open. 'I'm home,' Brian called.

'Riana, in here. Quick!' Paul pushed Riana inside the pantry and shut the door just as Brian came in. Brian's jaw dropped when he saw the ruined stove and icecream-covered floor.

'It's my fault, Dad. It ...' Paul stopped. He had no idea what to say next.

'It was a surprise for you,' Christine said. 'I was doing the washing up and making dinner ... and the wok caught on fire ... and while I was putting it out, I left the freezer open.' Christine looked as though she was about to cry.

Paul put his arm around her. 'I should have been keeping an eye on things.'

'I'm just glad that no-one got hurt,' Brian told them. 'Let's get this cleaned up, then we can go out for dinner.' He moved towards the pantry where the cleaning equipment was stored.

Paul dived in front of the door. 'Dad, this is our fault. We'll do the cleaning. You go and get some takeaway. We insist, don't we, Christine?'

Christine nodded.

'Chinese?' Brian asked.

'Great,' Paul said.

Brian went out and Paul breathed a sigh of relief. 'Chris, that was brilliant. Have I ever told you I love you?'

'No. And you'd better not start. Just remember our deal.'

Paul opened the pantry and Riana came out.

'You can stay in my room,' Christine said, 'and tell me all about the Spellbinders. Come on.' Christine took Riana's hand and headed for the door.

'Aren't you going to help me clean up?' Paul asked.

'I thought up the story.' Christine grinned at Paul and led Riana out of the kitchen. Paul groaned, grabbed a mop and started to clean up the mess.

When Brian got back with the takeaway food, Paul went upstairs to get Christine. There was laughter coming from her room. Paul hurried in and saw Christine and Riana sitting at the computer.

'Look, Paul,' Riana called excitedly. 'I can use a computer.'

On the screen, Riana's racing car crashed into Christine's and exploded in a ball of flame. Riana giggled.

'You've got to keep the noise down,' Paul hissed. 'If Dad finds out you're here, he might send you back to the hospital. Come on, sis, dinner's ready.'

Christine turned the volume down on the computer and followed Paul to the door.

'I'll sneak some food up to you later, Riana,' Paul said.

Riana nodded. As soon as Paul left, she turned back to the computer and started another race.

Paul awoke the next morning to see Brian standing over his bed with an armful of freshly ironed shirts. 'Paul, I'm leaving in a few minutes. Can you get Christine to school?'

'Yeah,' Paul mumbled but then he realised his father was carrying the shirts towards his wardrobe. The power suit was hanging inside. Paul scrambled out of bed and dived in front of the wardrobe door. 'I'll put those away.'

'How come every time I try to open a door around here, you're standing in the way?' Brian asked.

'Just trying to be helpful.' Paul smiled innocently.

His bemused father handed over the shirts and headed for the door. 'I'll get Christine up.'

Paul opened the wardrobe, then realised that Riana was sleeping in Christine's room!

Down the hallway, Christine screamed as Brian came through the door.

'Daddy,' she cried, huddling under her doona, 'I'm a young woman now. I might have been getting dressed.'

Brian suppressed a chuckle. 'Sorry. From now on, I'll knock first.'

Then Paul burst in.

'Knock,' Christine and Brian yelled together. They laughed at Paul's confusion.

'See you tonight,' Brian said, kissing Christine. 'Paul, can you pick up these groceries on the way home from school?'

He gave Paul a shopping list and some money. Once he had gone, Paul looked anxiously around the room. 'Where's Riana?'

A wall of soft toys under Christine's desk collapsed and Riana crawled out from a makeshift bed hidden behind them.

'How did you sleep?' Paul asked.

'Badly. I kept dreaming of my family. I wish I knew what was happening to them.'

'It's a pity you can't phone them,' Christine said.

'Maybe we can,' Paul told Riana. 'Well, sort

of. Alex and Katrina used a radio to contact your world. Maybe we can listen in on the Spellbinders and find out what's happening.'

Riana smiled gratefully.

'Christine, we have to get ready for school,' Paul said, heading for the door.

Riana went after him. 'I want to come with you. I want to see what school is like.'

'You can't. The teachers will want to know where you're from.'

'When you came to my world, I made up a story for you,' Riana reminded him. 'You can do the same for me.'

Alex opened his front door and was surprised to see Paul outside holding a bulging garbage bag.

'Dad almost saw the power suit this morning,' Paul said. 'Can I hide it here?'

'No problemo. I'll stash it in the garage.'

Paul followed Alex down the steps to the garage. Riana was waiting outside, wearing a pair of Paul's jeans and one of his windcheaters. They were too big for her so the legs and the sleeves were rolled up.

'What are you doing here?' Alex asked.

'I'm going to school.'

Alex shot Paul a worried look.

'Alex, meet my cousin Riana,' Paul said. 'She's from Iceland.'

Alex shook his head. 'It'll never work.'

'What?' Riana asked.

'It'll never work.'

'Yes,' she said, smiling broadly.

'What?' Alex asked, totally confused.

Paul laughed. 'It's simple. All Riana has to do is say "what" or "yes", then people will think she doesn't speak our language.'

Alex shook his head again and opened the garage door.

'Where's the radio you and Katrina used to contact Riana's world?' Paul asked him.

'Mr Kennett confiscated it.'

'We have to get it back.'

Mr Kennett was marking test papers in his school office. On the desk beside him was a half-empty packet of barley sugar. As he unwrapped another sweet, there was a knock at the door.

'What do you two want?' he snapped as Alex and Katrina came in.

'We'd like to apologise for our behaviour last week, sir,' Katrina said.

Alex nodded vigorously. 'Yeah, sir. We're sincerely and abjectly sorry. And we were wondering if we could have our radio back.' He pointed to the two-way radio sitting on a shelf behind the desk.

'You don't fool me, Katsonis,' the teacher said. 'If you're sorry, I'm a mongoose. You'll get it back at the end of term.' He popped the sweet into his mouth and went back to work.

Alex and Katrina went out. Paul and Riana were waiting in the corridor. 'The mongoose said no,' Alex told them.

The school bell started ringing and the corridor rapidly filled with students yelling and banging lockers open.

'Time to feed the animals,' Paul said.

'What animals?' Riana asked, looking warily around.

'He means us,' Katrina explained. 'We're about to be fed knowledge.'

'Will I learn to read today?' Riana asked eagerly.

'Sorry,' Paul said, 'it takes a bit longer than a day.'

Mr Kennett came out of his office carrying a bundle of papers. He glared at Alex as he passed.

'Why don't we get the radio now?' Riana asked.

'Kennett would suspect me right away,' Alex said.

'Don't worry,' Katrina told her, 'we'll think of something.'

Paul took Riana's hand. 'Come on. It's time to feed your brain.'

'And your stomach,' Alex added as they headed along the corridor. 'We've got home economics first.'

Ms Gibson was writing a recipe on the blackboard as Paul approached her with Riana.

'Ms Gibson, this is my cousin Riana. She's visiting from Iceland. Is it alright if she sits in on the class?'

'Of course.' Ms Gibson smiled at Riana.

'Welcome, Riana. I hope your English is better than my Icelandic.'

'Yes,' Riana said.

'Good.'

Riana smiled. 'What?'

Ms Gibson looked perplexed.

'Riana doesn't speak much English,' Paul explained. He quickly led Riana to a bench with a sink and a stove.

'OK,' Ms Gibson called. 'Mrs Smith is sick. So although I usually teach science, today I'm going to try my hand at another sort of chemistry. We're going to try out the formula for toffee.'

Half an hour later, the classroom was filled with the smell of burning toffee.

'We have to figure out a way to get into Kennett's office,' Paul whispered to Alex and Katrina.

'We need a Trojan horse,' Alex suggested.

Riana looked up from a saucepan of bubbling toffee. 'But a horse wouldn't fit in there.'

'It's not a real horse,' Alex explained. 'See,

the ancient Greeks were at war with the Trojans. They knew the Trojans really liked horses so they built a big wooden one and left it outside the city. When the Trojans took it inside, they discovered there was an army in it.'

'OK,' Paul said. 'We just have to figure out what Kennett likes.'

Katrina scooped up a spoonful of toffee from the saucepan. 'He's got a really sweet tooth.'

'Trojan toffee,' Alex exclaimed.

'Come in,' Mr Kennett called. The door opened and Paul wheeled in a trolley covered with a white table-cloth.

'We just made these in class, sir,' he said. 'I thought you might like some.'

Mr Kennett looked hungrily at the plate of toffees on the trolley. The bag of barley sugar beside him was empty. 'That's very kind of you, Paul.' He got up and went around the desk.

Paul tapped the trolley with his foot. Riana was crouched on the lower shelf, concealed by the table-cloth. She carefully crawled off the trolley and under the desk.

Mr Kennett selected a toffee, put it in his mouth and chewed. 'Mmmmm,' he mumbled, 'delicious.'

Crouched under the desk, Riana looked up at the two-way radio on the shelf. She couldn't reach it without the teacher seeing her. Paul realised her predicament and, picking up the plate, he moved away from the trolley.

'Take some home with you, sir.' He held out the plate.

Mr Kennett turned away from the desk and reached for the toffee. Riana got to her feet and grabbed the radio.

'Excuse me, sir,' a girl said from the door.

'What?' Mr Kennett asked.

Paul watched helplessly as the teacher started to turn. Behind him, Riana ran to the open window and dived through.

'A girl just dived out your window,' the stunned girl said.

Mr Kennett went to the window and stuck his head out. He saw Alex and Katrina outside in the yard. 'Did you two just see a girl jump out of my window?'

'No, sir,' Alex replied.

Mr Kennett's eyes swept the playground, then he disappeared back into his office. Riana was huddled against the wall under the window ledge. Alex gave her the thumbs up. Riana grinned and held up the radio.

Hidden amongst the trees at the edge of the school playing field, Paul, Riana and Katrina watched eagerly as Alex switched on the two-way radio. There was only the sound of static. Paul took the radio and pressed the talk button. 'This is Paul calling the Regents. Can you hear me? ... Lukan? Marna? Please answer me.'

There was no response. Paul saw the look of despair on Riana's face. 'They're probably still repairing the Summoning Tower,' he reassured her. 'We'll try again later.'

'I should take you shopping,' Katrina suggested. 'That always cheers me up. Got any money, Paul?'·

'Yeah. But it's for groceries.'

'Riana can't wear your clothes all the time,' Katrina said. 'She looks like a dag. We'll be back before the end of lunchtime.'

Katrina held out her hand and Paul reluctantly gave her the money.

The shopping mall fascinated Riana. She ran excitedly from shop to shop looking at all the things for sale. She didn't even know what half of them were for.

'There are so many different types of clothes,' she marvelled.

'People like to have a choice about what they wear,' Katrina explained. 'It's called fashion.'

'In my world,' Riana said, 'most people just have one set of clothes. My mother is lucky. She has two dresses.'

'Two? My mother's got at least thirty.'

'Thirty?' Riana echoed in amazement.

'Yeah. And she still has trouble deciding what to wear.'

They both laughed. Katrina took Riana into a jeans shop. When they left, Riana was proudly wearing a bright floral-print dress and a denim jacket. She carried Paul's clothes in a shopping bag.

'You look great,' Katrina told her. 'We'd better get back to school.'

As they crossed the mall, Riana noticed a girl crouched on the pavement, drawing on a piece of canvas.

'Josie?' Riana called.

Josie looked up and grinned when she saw Riana coming towards her.

'I told you there was no begging allowed here.'

Josie looked round and saw a security guard coming towards her. 'I'm not begging,' she protested.

'Get out of here or I'll call the cops,' the guard threatened. Josie angrily rolled up her canvas.

'Where's Ben?' Riana asked.

'He's sick. I was just trying to get money to buy new batteries for his Gameboy.'

Riana turned to Katrina. 'Is there any money left?'

'Paul said not to spend it all,' Katrina reminded her.

'Josie's a friend. She needs it.'

Katrina gave the remainder of the money to Riana who handed the notes to Josie. The girl took them gratefully.

'I told you, no begging,' the guard said.

Josie backed away. 'We found a new place in an old warehouse down by the harbour,' she quickly told Riana. 'Come and see us. Look for the dragon.' She turned and ran.

'How come you know her?' Katrina asked Riana as they left the mall.

'Josie helped me when I was lost. She's trying to find her father but she doesn't even know his name.'

'Isn't it on her birth certificate?' Katrina asked.

Riana looked at her blankly. 'What's a birth certificate?'

'Slow down, Bron,' Correon called breathlessly.

Bron was striding along the forest trail, the bag containing the video-camera swinging from his shoulder. 'I want my family back,' he replied, not slackening his pace.

Zander and Correon struggled to keep up with him. Zander was carrying Arla on his back. 'Listen,' Arla cried.

The crackling of electricity could be heard above the forest sounds.

Bron pushed his way up an overgrown slope and stopped. The stone walls of the Spellbinder castle stood before him. Bolts of power sparked around the pylon on top of the central tower. Muscular, leather-clad sentries stood guard at the castle gate.

Correon and Zander struggled up the slope to join Bron. 'I hate this place,' Zander said, remembering the time he had spent in the cold cell in the castle.

'But it's beautiful,' Arla whispered.

'And dangerous,' Correon reminded them.

'What do we do now?' Zander asked.

'Da?' Arla suddenly called.

Zander and Correon turned and saw Bron plunging down the thickly wooded slope towards the castle.

'Bron, wait,' Correon shouted.

Bron didn't stop.

'So can anyone in your world become a Spellbinder?' Katrina asked Riana as they came out of school at the end of the day.

'First you must become an Apprentice,' Riana explained. 'Then you study with a Spellbinder until you have learnt all the secrets —how to read, how to use a power suit ...'

'I can read already,' Katrina interrupted. 'And if Paul can use a power suit, so can I. I could be a Spellbinder.'

Riana laughed at the idea.

'Can I come round and try out the power suit?' Katrina asked Paul.

'No way. It's dangerous!'

'I'll be careful.'

'No.'

'It's not fair,' Katrina complained. 'You and Alex have seen it work. Why can't I? '

'Because I don't want anyone to find out about it,' Paul said. 'I had to hide it in Alex's garage so my dad wouldn't see it.'

'But I ...,' Katrina started.

'No!'

Katrina stormed away.

'You really upset her,' Alex said to Paul.

'She'll be alright.'

'Are we going home now?' Riana asked.

'I can't,' Paul said. 'Alex and I have rugby practice.'

'What's rugby practice?'

A short while later, Riana stood at the edge of the playing field, watching a group of muddy boys throw a leather ball around. The ball flew from a pack and Paul grabbed it. He tried to run but Giannos tackled him and Paul crashed to the ground. Riana ran onto the field, leaped on Giannos, wrestled him to the ground and put him in a headlock.

'Get off me,' Giannos yelled.

Paul struggled to his feet. 'Riana, let him go!'

Riana released the angry boy.

'Sorry, Giannos. She didn't know it was a game,' Paul said. 'They don't play rugby in Iceland.'

Giannos walked away, embarrassed at being beaten by a girl.

'That was really dumb,' Paul said to Riana.

'I thought you needed help,' Riana protested.

'Well, I didn't. It's just a game.'

'Can I play?'

'Girls don't play rugby.'

'Why?' Riana said with a grin. 'Are the boys afraid the girls might win?'

'Don't be stupid,' Paul snapped.

Stung by his answer, Riana walked away.

'Riana, I'm sorry.'

Riana kept walking. 'I'll see you back at your home,' she called over her shoulder.

The coach blew his whistle and the game resumed.

'Paul,' Alex yelled.

Paul looked round and Alex passed him the ball. As he caught it, Giannos leaped on him again. Paul hit the ground with a groan. Riana didn't look back.

The sentries, Mort and Borin, were standing by the guard hut at the castle gate when Bron strode out of the trees. 'What do you want here?' Mort asked.

Before Bron could answer, Gryvon ran out of the guard hut, yelling, 'That's him!'

Mort and Borin seized Bron. Gryvon swaggered up to him. 'Have you got the picture box?' he demanded.

Bron held the camera bag tightly to his chest. 'I'm not giving it to you.'

'Take him inside,' Gryvon ordered.

Hidden in the trees, Correon, Zander and Arla watched anxiously as the sentries hustled Bron into the castle.

Ashka looked up from her desk as the door of her apartment opened and a guard thrust Bron inside. Gryvon strutted in after them.

'This is Bron,' he said triumphantly to Ashka. 'He walked into my trap and I captured him.'

'I gave myself up,' Bron said.

'Silence,' Gryvon bellowed.

Bron ignored him and turned to Ashka. 'Where are my wife and son?'

'Do you have the picture box?'

Bron held out the bag.

'Show me,' Ashka demanded.

'I want to see my family first.'

'You'll do as I tell you,' the Spellbinder

shouted. She snatched the bag from Bron and opened it. Inside was a large rock.

'Where is it?' Ashka screamed.

Dressed in his Marauder disguise, Zander stepped out of the trees and let out a roar. Borin stared at the hideous green creature lumbering towards the castle gates.

'Mort,' he screeched, 'Is that a Marauder?'

Mort came out of the guard hut and gaped at the approaching figure. 'What do we do?'

'There's a reward for catching a Marauder,' Borin reminded him. 'This one isn't very big.'

They began to move hesitantly forward. Zander turned off the track and ran into the forest. The sentries pulled clubs from their belts and raced after him.

Once they were gone, Correon and Arla emerged from the trees on the other side of the track and ran towards the castle gate. Correon was carrying the video-camera.

Katrina slowly opened the door of Alex's garage and peered inside. 'Hello?' she called.

There was no reply. Katrina came in, shut the door and began searching the cluttered garage. Under the old blanket in the corner, she found a garbage bag. The power suit was inside.

'Hey, Katrina,' Nick said, 'what ya doing?'

Katrina whirled around and saw Alex's brother coming through the door. She quickly closed the bag. 'Nothing,' she stammered. 'I just brought something round for Alex.'

'He's not home yet. You can leave it with me.'

'No,' Katrina said, 'it's OK. I'll see him tomorrow.'

Katrina's heart was thumping as she picked up the garbage bag and hurried out. She was going to experience the Spellbinder's power.

Maran sat shivering in the cold stone cell, watching Jal play with Correon's magic stones. She was trying not think about what

Ashka might do to them. Then the door clanged open and a guard shoved a figure into the cell.

'Bron,' Maran cried.

As Bron embraced his wife and son, Ashka came in.

'Now tell me where the picture box is,' she commanded, 'or I'll take you all straight to the Wastelands.'

Bron stared defiantly at Ashka and said nothing.

'Forgive me, Spellbinder,' Gryvon called from the door, 'the Regents want to see you.'

'You'd better have an answer by the time I get back,' Ashka warned Bron. She went out and Gryvon slammed the cell door.

Bron started to laugh. Maran stared at him, wondering if her husband had gone mad.

'Don't worry,' Bron said. 'We're going to be alright.'

Ashka strode into the Regents' chamber and bowed to Lukan and Marna.

'So you think we're fools, do you?' Lukan asked, barely able to contain his rage.

'Of course not,' Ashka replied warily. 'Who told you that?'

'The Regents are fools,' Ashka heard herself say.

She whirled around and was shocked to see Correon and Arla. Correon was holding the video-camera. 'How did you survive the Wastelands?' Ashka asked.

Correon smiled. Ashka's eyes widened in horror as she saw herself on the camera's screen.

'You want the gunpowder to use against the Regents,' Paul's recorded voice said. 'You want to rule the Spellbinders.'

On the screen, Ashka smiled. 'Very perceptive,' she said.

Correon stopped the tape. The Regents stared accusingly at Ashka.

'This is all a mistake,' she spluttered. 'I haven't done anything wrong.'

'She burnt my house down,' Arla cried.

'Don't worry,' Marna gently told her. 'She'll never harm anyone again.'

Ashka turned and raced out of the chamber.

'Get my power suit and meet me in the

courtyard,' she yelled to Gryvon who was waiting outside. Before he could ask why, she disappeared down the corridor.

Ashka raced into the castle courtyard. 'Bring my horse and open the gate,' she yelled. Two guards ran to do her bidding.

As she mounted, Gryvon came out of the castle, carrying her power suit. As he hurried towards Ashka, Marna appeared on a balcony above the courtyard. 'Stop them,' she cried. 'Close the gates.'

The guard who was opening the gate began closing it. The other tackled Gryvon and the power suit fell to the ground. Before Ashka could get it, more guards ran out of the castle. Ashka wheeled her horse round and galloped towards the gates. The guard stood in her way and was knocked aside as she rode through. Two Apprentices leaped into the moat as Ashka thundered across the bridge. Correon and Lukan joined Marna on the balcony and watched helplessly as Ashka galloped into the forest.

Below them, Mort and Borin dragged Zander through the gate into the courtyard.

He was still in his Marauder disguise.

'Leave him,' Correon shouted. 'He's my friend.'

Mort and Borin stared in shock at Correon: the old Regent was supposed to be dead.

'Do as the Regent says,' Lukan ordered.

The sentries quickly released Zander.

'Would you like to meet a Marauder?' Correon asked Lukan. Zander threw back the hood of his disguise and Lukan was amazed to see that the fearsome Marauder was just a young man.

After leaving Paul at the school, Riana made her way through the winding streets, trying to remember the way back to his home.

'Riana,' Christine shouted from the other side of the street. Riana waved back and hurried towards her.

A police car was parked at the kerb. Inside, two policemen stared at Riana. One checked a clipboard, then got out of the car and approached her. 'Is your name Riana?'

Riana started to back away.

'It's alright,' the policeman said. 'We're just going to take you back to the hospital.'

As he tried to take her arm, Riana dodged and leaped onto the bonnet of the police car. She ran over the car roof, leaped off the back and raced up the road.

'Stop,' the policeman yelled and took off after her.

The policeman in the car quickly started his engine. 'You wait there,' he shouted at Christine. The car did a U-turn and roared after Riana.

Christine watched Riana disappear into a lane, pursued by the police, then turned and ran in the other direction.

'So what are you going to do about Riana?' Alex asked Paul as they stood outside Alex's house, still in their rugby gear.

'I'm not sure,' Paul admitted. 'I guess when things have calmed down a bit, I'll try and tell my dad the truth. See you tomorrow.'

Paul headed back down the street. As Alex started to climb the steps to his front door, he heard a muffled voice from inside his bag. 'Paul,' he shouted.

Paul and Alex hurried into the garage and Alex pulled the radio from his bag.

'What did you hear?' Paul asked.

'I dunno. A voice.'

Suddenly, Correon's voice came from the radio. 'Paul, this is Correon. Can you hear me, Paul? Please answer.'

Paul grabbed the radio from Alex.

'Correon,' he yelled into it. 'You're alive!'

'Kurn and Zander rescued me from the Wastelands,' Correon explained. 'I'm back in the castle.'

'Paul,' a woman's voice said, 'Is Riana with you?'

'Maran?' Paul asked in surprise. 'Correon, what's going on?'

'The Regents saw your tape,' Correon explained. 'Ashka is gone from the castle.'

Paul cheered. 'Riana's fine, Maran. She misses you. She can't wait to get home.'

'The Summoning Tower has been repaired,' Correon said. 'You can bring Riana home as soon as you like.'

'I'll contact you when we're ready,' Paul told him. 'I'm really glad you're safe.'

'So am I,' Correon said.

Paul turned off the radio and grinned at Alex. Everything was going to be alright.

'When are we going to do it?' Alex asked.

'What's wrong with now? Get the power suit.'

Alex went to the corner of the garage and lifted the blanket. He looked at Paul in horror. 'It's gone!'

Run!

Alex and Paul stared at the place where the power suit had been.

'Are you sure you didn't move it?' Paul asked.

'Yes!'

'Well who else knew the power suit was here?'

The door opened and Nick came into the garage, whistling. Alex stormed over to him. 'What have you done with the power suit?'

'The what?' Nick asked.

'Er ... my Electroman costume. That suit thing you saw me hiding.'

'I didn't touch your dumb costume,' Nick said. He pushed past Alex and went to the bench where he opened his toolbox.

'You're the only other person who's seen it,' Alex insisted.

'What about your girlfriend?' Nick asked.

Now Alex was confused. 'What girlfriend?'

'Katrina. She was here earlier. She was going ...'

Before he could finish, Paul and Alex raced out of the garage.

Katrina finished buckling up the power suit and admired her reflection in her bedroom mirror. 'I am Katrina, the Spellbinder,' she said in an imperious voice.

She ran her hand over the copper fittings, looking for a switch to turn the suit on. Unable to find one, she opened the power-stone housings on the belt. One contained a dull-looking stone; the other was empty. Katrina looked into the garbage bag. A gleaming stone lay inside. She picked it up and smiled as she slid it into the housing.

Paul and Alex were breathless by the time they reached Katrina's house. They ran across the front yard and peered through the study window. Mr Muggleton was working at his computer. The faint sound of classical music came from a stereo.

'Everything looks OK,' Alex whispered.

'It won't be if Katrina gets the suit going,' Paul reminded him. He went to the front door and rang the bell. Mr Muggleton opened it.

'Is Katrina here?' Paul asked. 'We have to see her.'

Mr Muggleton glared at Alex. 'I thought I told you to stay away from my daughter.'

Upstairs, Katrina sighed and folded her arms. She still couldn't get the power suit working. She decided to return it before the boys noticed it was gone. As Katrina unfolded her arms, the copper plates on her wrists touched and a spark jumped between them.

As Mr Muggleton started to close the front door, the music in the study suddenly became deafening. The electric doorbell started ringing and the porch light flashed on and off. A shocked Mr Muggleton ran towards his study, leaving the front door open.

'It's the power suit,' Paul said. He grabbed Alex and pulled him into the house.

In her bedroom, Katrina was petrified. Energy was crackling over the power suit, her bedroom lights were flashing on and off and music blared from the clock-radio beside her bed. Then the light globe in the ceiling exploded and Katrina screamed.

Paul and Alex burst in. Paul ripped open the housing on the power suit belt and wrenched out the powerstone. The suit went dead.

'I'm sorry,' Katrina wailed in the sudden silence. 'I just wanted to see it work. I didn't realise it would do that.'

'Well, now you know,' Paul snapped. 'Take it off. I can't believe you could be so stupid!' He angrily started to undo the buckles of the power suit.

'Take it easy, mate,' Alex said. 'She said she was sorry.'

'She could have ruined everything,' Paul replied.

'We spoke to the Spellbinders,' Alex explained to Katrina. 'Riana can go home.'

'That's great. When you take her back, I want to go with you. I want to see her world too.'

'Haven't you caused enough trouble?' Paul asked.

'If it wasn't for me,' Katrina reminded him, 'you'd still be trapped in Riana's world.'

'She's right, Paul,' Alex said.

Before Paul could reply, Mr Muggleton called from downstairs. 'Katrina, are you OK?'

'If I don't answer,' Katrina said softly, 'Dad'll come up here and see the suit.'

Paul considered his options. 'Alright, you can come.'

Katrina smiled. 'I'm fine,' she called.

Paul raced home to give Riana the good news. He ran into the house calling her name.

'Paul,' Christine called softly from the loungeroom.

Paul hurried in and saw his sister peeking out from behind the sofa. 'What are you doing there? Where's Riana?'

'The police chased her.'

Paul was horrified. 'What? Did she get away?'

'I don't know,' Christine whimpered. 'The police told me to stay put but I didn't want to be caught so I ran too. I'm scared. I don't want to go to gaol.'

'It's OK. You won't go to gaol,' Paul said gently. He helped Christine up. 'I'm going to look for Riana. If she comes back, hide her in your room. Tell her Correon's alive and she can go home.'

Paul hurried out.

Riana trudged along the edge of the harbour. She was too frightened to go back to Paul's in case the police were waiting, so she had decided to try and find Josie, her only other friend in this world. She knew Josie was living by the harbour but the harbour was huge and now it was getting dark. An enormous bridge arched above her, carrying hundreds of cars. She wondered where they were all going and why they had to get there so fast.

Ahead was a row of old warehouses built on a pier over the water. As Riana walked among the pillars supporting the buildings, she noticed something painted in bright colours on a door: it was Josie's dragon. Riana pushed the door open and went in.

The old warehouse was a vast gloomy building. The walls were made of slats like the barn in Clayhill but the derelict building smelt damp and the floor was filthy and littered with broken glass. Riana made her way through a maze of empty rooms. As she passed a doorway, she heard a cough. Riana looked in.

In the corner of the room was a mattress, piled with sacking. The electronic beeping of a Gameboy came from beneath it. Riana tiptoed over and lifted the sacking. Ben was underneath. He screamed. Josie raced in, brandishing a wooden pole.

'Josie,' Ben yelled, 'it's Riana.'

Josie lowered the pole and smiled. 'I'm glad you came. You're our first visitor.'

'The police were chasing me,' Riana explained.

Josie ran to the window and looked out warily. 'Did they follow you?'

'No. They wanted to take me back to the hospital. Then I remembered your directions.'

Ben started to cough again. Josie picked up a bottle and poured some red syrup into a plastic measuring cup.

'Is he sick?' Riana asked. Josie nodded. 'Why don't you take him to a Healer?'

'A what?'

'A ... a hospital?'

'Because when we give our names, they'll find out we're runaways,' Josie explained. 'They'll keep Ben there and I'll never see him again. Benny, drink this.'

Ben drank the medicine. Riana watched with concern as Josie sat beside him on the mattress and rubbed his back.

'It'll be OK, Benny,' she said encouragingly. 'It'll be OK.'

Riana could see that Josie was putting on a brave front.

Paul realised that there was no point searching for Riana in the dark. He told himself that if she could survive alone in the forests of her world, spending the night in the suburbs of Sydney would be easy. As he headed wearily towards his house, Paul saw his father's car in the driveway and groaned. He carefully opened the front door and crept in.

Christine looked up from a book as Paul peered around the loungeroom door. 'Did you find her?' she asked anxiously.

Paul shook his head and put his fingers to lips but Brian came out of the kitchen. 'Do you realise what time it is?' he snapped. 'Where have you been?'

'Um ... I was at Alex's.'

'No you weren't. I rang his mother. Where's the shopping?'

'I forgot to do it,' Paul said meekly.

'Then where's the money I gave you?'

'I ... er ... lost it.'

His father sighed with exasperation. 'Paul, what's going on? If you're in some kind of trouble, tell me. Maybe I can help.'

'You can't.'

'How do you know if you won't give me a chance?'

Paul said nothing.

'Paul, I know you've had a hard time but I'm getting pretty fed up with you. You're part of a family. Try thinking about somebody else for a change.'

Paul was too exhausted and worried about

129

Riana to argue. He walked past his father and started to climb the stairs.

'Paul,' Brian yelled at his son's back.

'I'll go and talk to him,' Christine said. She hurried upstairs, knocked softly on his door and went in. Paul was lying on his bed, staring at the ceiling.

'Maybe you should tell Dad the truth,' she suggested.

Paul shook his head despairingly. 'Dad still thinks I'm nuts. Why hasn't Riana come back? What if the police got her?'

'Riana's smart,' Christine assured him. 'She would have got away.'

Josie pulled a rotten slat from the warehouse wall and carried it over to the small fire which crackled on the concrete floor. Riana and Ben sat on the mattress by the fire. Riana was playing with Ben's Gameboy.

'Straight on. Now jump,' Ben shouted. 'Now through there. That's it!'

There was a tinny fanfare from the Gameboy and Riana grinned. 'I rescued the princess. It was easy that time.'

'That's only the beginner's level,' Ben explained. 'There's eight more.' He started to cough.

'That's enough, Benny,' Josie said gently. 'Time for bed.'

'Goodnight, Riana,' Ben said as his sister tucked him under the sacking.

'Dream well, Ben,' Riana replied. 'I'll get you a surprise for breakfast.'

Riana began sharpening the end of Josie's wooden pole with her knife. Josie kissed Ben goodnight, then joined Riana by the fire.

'Is he getting any better?' Riana asked.

Josie sadly shook her head. 'We can't go on living like this. I'm never going to find my dad. I don't even know where to start looking.'

Riana smiled. 'I think I do.'

Brian and Christine were eating breakfast when Paul came in, dressed for school. 'Listen, about last night ...' Brian began.

'Sorry, Dad,' Paul interrupted. 'I'll repay you the money.'

Brian gave him a conciliatory smile. 'The money's not important. I'm worried about us.

I'm sorry I got angry. Sometimes I'm not too good at this father stuff.'

'Maybe you should get married again,' Christine said.

Brian snorted. 'Where would I find the time? Anyway, I don't know any single women.'

'Gina's not married,' Christine said eagerly. 'She likes you.'

Brian gaped. 'Gina?'

'She does,' Christine insisted, 'doesn't she, Paul?'

'Uh, yeah,' Paul replied, remembering the deal he'd made with his sister. 'She thinks you're a real spunk. Bye.' He hurried out.

Brian stared in disbelief at Christine. 'Gina?'

An old man stood at the end of the pier, pulling in a fishing line. A lump of seaweed dangled from the end. He stared in surprise when he saw Riana wading into the water by the pier. She was carrying Josie's pole.

Riana stood waist deep in the water, the pole poised in her hand like a spear. Her eyes were fixed on something under the surface. Then she plunged the pole into the water. She pulled it out, a fish wriggling on the sharpened end. On the shore, Josie and Ben clapped. The old man looked at the seaweed on his fish-hook and shook his head.

Back in the warehouse, Riana, Josie and Ben sat around the fire, pulling succulent morsels off the fish that was roasting on a spit.

'What's a birth certificate?' Ben asked.

'It's a piece of paper that tells when you were born and who your parents are,' Riana said, recalling Katrina's explanation.

'But if we don't know where Josie's dad is,' Ben asked, 'how are we going to find the certificate?'

'There's a copy in a special building called a registry,' Josie said. 'It'll be in my name. Let's go.' Steam hissed as she poured a bucket of water over the fire.

The Births, Marriages and Deaths Registry was a big, grey building in the city. Josie, Ben and Riana rode the lift to the third floor. Josie went to a counter in a large, crowded office and asked for a copy of her birth certificate. A clerk told her to wait.

'It's taking so long,' Josie said after twenty minutes had passed. 'What if they can't find it?'

'Rats might have eaten it,' Ben suggested.

The clerk waved to Josie. She got up and went to the counter. Riana and Ben followed.

'Here's your birth certificate,' the clerk said, holding out a sheet of paper. 'That will be forty-five dollars.'

'How much?' Josie asked in horror.

'Forty-five dollars. That's thirty for the certificate and ...'

'I don't really need the certificate,' Josie explained. 'I just want to see what my father's name is.'

'That's against regulations,' the clerk said. He put the paper under the counter. 'Next.'

Riana and Ben followed Josie away. 'I'll never get that much cash together,' Josie moaned. 'We're stuffed.'

'No, we're not.' Riana put her arms around them and whispered her plan.

'What about that money you owe me?' Josie suddenly bellowed at Riana.

'I gave it to you,' Riana yelled back.

Everyone in the office looked at them. Ben

moved towards the counter.

'You did not,' Josie shouted. 'I want it now. I need it.' She reached for Riana's pocket but Riana backed away. 'Give it to me,' Josie demanded.

Riana raced around the office, pushing past people as Josie tried to catch her.

'Stop that, you two,' the clerk shouted. He hurried out from behind the counter. As he tried to grab the girls, Ben sneaked behind the counter and looked at the certificate.

'Take your argument outside,' the clerk told Josie and Riana as he hustled them out the door.

'Bye,' Ben said cheekily as he ran past the clerk.

'Well?' Josie asked Ben in the lift.

'His name's Peter,' Ben said.

'Peter what?'

Ben carefully spelt the name out letter by letter. 'E.R.I.K.S.E.N.'

'Eriksen,' Josie crowed. 'I'm Josie Eriksen!' She hugged Ben and Riana. 'Let's go and find my dad.'

Josie ripped a page from a telephone

directory in the foyer of the building. She bought a street map and after a couple of bus rides, the kids were walking along a suburban street. Josie checked the address from the directory page and stopped outside a large house.

'This is the first P. Eriksen in the book,' she announced, looking nervously at the well-kept garden. 'What am I going to say if it's him?'

'Just say who you are,' Riana suggested.

'What if he doesn't want me?'

'Then we'll think of something else. But you have to try.'

Josie gathered her courage, then went up the path to the front door and knocked. The door opened and Josie smiled. 'Hi,' she blurted out. 'I'm your long-lost daughter, Josie.' She stopped when she realised that the man in the doorway was Aboriginal. 'Sorry,' she said. 'Wrong house.' The bemused Koori watched as Josie raced back to the street.

The second Eriksen was a nun and the third one slammed the door in her face. Discouraged, Josie rang a fourth doorbell but no-one was home. She trudged despondently back to the gate where Riana and Ben were waiting. 'This is hopeless,' she said and started walking away.

'Why don't we leave a note saying who you are and where we live?' Ben suggested. 'Then if this one is your dad, he can come and find us.'

'We can do the same if any of the others aren't home,' Riana said.

Josie sighed. 'It's worth a try.' She opened the letter box, took out an envelope addressed to P. Eriksen and started writing a message on the back.

Paul and Alex walked despondently towards Paul's house. They had skipped school and spent the day searching for Riana without success. Paul knew he couldn't go to the police but didn't know what else to do.

As they reached the drive, Alex pointed to something drawn in white chalk on the wall of Paul's house. Paul recognised the two intertwined snakes. 'That's a Spellbinder sign,' he told Alex excitedly. 'Riana's been here!'

He looked around and saw a smaller Spellbinder sign chalked on the pavement.

Below it, an arrow pointed along the street. 'She's left a trail. Come on.'

The trail of signs led Paul and Alex to the derelict warehouses by the harbour. Paul saw a Spellbinder sign chalked on a door beneath a drawing of a dragon. He pushed the door open.

Alex sniffed. 'I smell cooking.' He led the way into the gloomy building.

Alex followed his nose through the warehouse to where they found Riana and Ben roasting a fish over the fire. Paul put his fingers to his lips and gestured to Alex that they should sneak up on her.

As the boys crept towards Riana, Josie appeared behind them. 'Get out or I'll gut you,' she yelled, menacing them with Riana's spear. The boys backed away.

'Josie, no,' Riana called, 'that's Paul.'

Josie lowered the spear and Paul hurried over to Riana. 'I've got great news,' he said. 'The radio's working. I spoke to Maran. Your family's safe. And Correon's alive! He told me the Summoning Tower's been fixed.'

'I can go home!' Riana cried as she hugged Paul.

'Can I have one of those too?' Alex asked cheekily. Riana hugged him.

'We'll get a train up to the cave in the morning,' Paul said. 'We just need to keep you safe till then.'

'Riana's safe here,' Josie said firmly.

'Josie and Ben are my friends,' Riana explained. 'I'm happy here. And I want to see if Josie's father turns up. We've been looking for him.'

'OK,' Paul agreed. 'I'll be back in the morning. Early. Please be here. This could be your only chance to get home.'

'Where exactly is your home?' Josie asked Riana after Paul and Alex left.

'I told you. The Spellbinders' land. It's in another world.'

Ben grinned. 'I knew you were telling the truth.'

Josie shook her head. 'This is too weird.'

Dressed in a servant's uniform, Gryvon sat on the floor of Correon's apartment. He scowled as he slowly rubbed a cloth over Ashka's power suit.

'When you've finished polishing that,' Correon said. 'You can do these.' He dumped a large pile of boots on the floor. Gryvon gritted his teeth. 'Yes, Regent.'

He looked up in surprise as Paul's voice came from Correon's Eyestone. 'Correon, it's Paul. Can you hear me?'

'Yes, Paul,' Correon replied. 'Is Riana ready to come home?'

'Yes. I think's she's had enough of my world. Can you be at the Clayhill Summoning Tower at midday tomorrow? I need you to open the doorway from your side.'

'I'll leave straightaway,' Correon promised.

'Thanks, Correon. I'll see you tomorrow.'

Gryvon quickly resumed polishing the power suit, pretending that he hadn't been listening.

Ben and Riana were whirling sets of newly made bolas around their heads. Across the warehouse floor, a row of tins were lined up.

'Easy ... easy,' Riana instructed. 'And ... now!'

The cords weighted with stones flew through the air and knocked the tins over.

'Josie,' Ben yelled, 'I did it!'

'Great,' Josie murmured without enthusiasm, from beside the fire.

As Ben collected the bolas, Riana sat by Josie. 'Don't give up hope. Your father might still turn up.'

'Even if he does get the note, he probably won't want us,' Josie said. 'He walked out on Mum. He probably hates kids.' She looked up as car headlights splashed on the warehouse wall.

'Maybe that's him,' Ben said.

Outside, car doors slammed, followed by the sound of teenage laughter and breaking glass.

'Douse the fire,' Josie hissed.

Riana smothered the fire with dirt and hid in the shadows with Josie and Ben.

The sound of footsteps echoed through the building, then three figures came into the room. One of them flicked on a torch, revealing the faces of a twelve-year-old boy and two tough-looking teenagers. The boy, Terry, looked anxiously around.

'Do I have to do this, Bazza?' he asked the teenager with the torch.

'Do you wanna be part of the gang or not, little brother?' Bazza said. Terry nodded. 'Then you have to pass the initiation test. And that means spending the night here ... alone ... with the ghost of Cannibal Tom.'

'And his six unsuspecting dinner guests,' his mate, Tommo, added in a deep menacing voice.

Bazza sneaked up behind Terry and howled in his ear. The boy yelled in fright and stumbled away, losing his balance. He fell backwards onto the dirt-covered fire.

'I'm on fire,' he screeched, leaping to his feet and beating at the smoking seat of his pants.

Bazza kicked at the fire, exposing the glowing coals. He looked around and saw the bedding, food and utensils. 'Someone's living here,' he said.

'The initiation's changed, Terry,' Tommo smirked. 'Trash the place.'

Spurred on by his burnt bum, Terry savagely kicked over the table. The cooking utensils clattered across the floor. Bazza and Tommo applauded. Terry overturned the mattress and Ben's tattered book fell out of the sacking. He started ripping it up, throwing the pages on the coals of the fire. They burst into flames.

Furious, Riana started to move forward but Josie held her back. 'No,' she whispered, 'I've got a better idea.'

She picked up a piece of metal and scraped it against the floor, making a loud, eerie sound. Terry stopped what he was doing and looked nervously around. Josie scraped the metal again and Ben started to moan into an empty tin can. His voice echoed weirdly.

'It's Cannibal Tom,' Terry wailed and bolted out the door.

'Who's there?' Tommo said warily. 'Come out!' He saw Ben's Gameboy on the floor and picked it up.

'Put it back,' Josie yelled.

Tommo looked round and saw her step out of the darkness, holding the spear. He grinned menacingly. 'Make me.'

Riana's bolas flew out of the darkness and knocked the Gameboy from Tommo's hand. The surprised teenager spun around and saw Riana. She was whirling the other set of bolas.

Josie raised her spear. 'Get out!'

'Come on,' Bazza said, 'they're crazy.'

'I won't forget this,' Tommo snarled as they backed out of the door. Josie, Riana and Ben laughed with relief.

Christine turned away from the loungeroom window as a car pulled into Paul's driveway. 'Dad's here.'

On the sofa, Paul and Alex looked at each other nervously.

'What if he doesn't go for it?' Alex asked.

'He has to,' Paul said. 'We've got to get Riana to the cave by midday.' He stood up as Brian came through the door. 'Hi, Dad. Alex and his father are going on a fishing trip tomorrow and they've asked me to come along. We'll have to leave pretty early.'

'Yeah,' Alex added, 'Pop knows this place down the coast. He's getting the tackle ready now. We'll have Paul back tomorrow night.

With all the snapper you can eat.'

'Sounds great,' Brian said.

Paul smiled. 'Thanks, Dad.'

'I'd like to speak to your father first,' Brian told Alex. 'What's your number?'

'Pop's not home yet,' Alex said quickly.

'I thought you said he was getting the tackle ready.'

'Yeah. I did, didn't I,' Alex spluttered. 'I'd better get back and help him. Paul can give you the number.'

Alex raced out. Brian picked up the phone and looked at Paul.

'It's er ... 309 4781,' Paul said.

Brian dialled the number. A woman's voice answered. 'Dr William's surgery.'

Alex scrambled over the fence at the rear of Paul's house and started to run across the garden which backed on to it. He had to get home before Mr Reynolds spoke to his father and discovered that there was no fishing trip. As Alex raced across the yard, a large dog started to bark. Alex looked back fearfully. 'Nice doggy,' he called as he sprinted for the fence.

Paul scratched his head and looked at his father. 'It could be 4187 ... or 7481. I'm sorry, Dad, I always get it mixed up.'

Brian hung up the phone. 'I'll look it up.'

'I'll do it.' Christine grabbed the telephone book before her father could get to it.

'L ... M ... N,' she recited, slowly leafing through the pages.

'Katsonis begins with K,' Brian said.

Christine looked at the phone book and laughed. 'Silly me. Wrong book.'

There was the sound of growling and cloth tearing as Alex clambered over his back fence. 'Get off, you rotten mongrel,' he yelled.

He hauled himself over the fence and dropped to the ground, panting. Half his trouser leg was gone. A phone started ringing inside his house.

'That's for me,' Alex yelled and raced inside. He came back out with the cordless phone and pushed the talk button.

'Stavros Katsonis speaking,' he said in a deep voice. 'Mr Reynolds, hello .... Your Paul is good boy. Almost as good as my Alex ... Yes, I did invite Paul to come fishing ... Now don't you worry. Paul won't drown. And if he does, we'll dry him out good before we bring him home.' Alex laughed heartily.

Brian put down the phone and turned to Paul. 'OK. You can go.'

Paul breathed a sigh of relief. 'Thanks, Dad,'

Brian smiled. He'd done something right at last.

Riana, Josie and Ben walked back along the pier towards the warehouse. Ben held a plastic bucket containing the results of another early morning fishing expedition.

'Six fish,' he marvelled. 'If you stayed with us, Riana, we'd never have to buy food.'

From the other side of the building came the rumble of a powerful engine. Josie looked up as a battered red car appeared around the corner. Through the windscreen, she could see Bazza and Tommo.

'It's those mongrels from last night,' Josie warned. With a squeal of tyres, the car accelerated towards them. 'Run!'

147

Reunions

Riana, Josie and Ben fled along the wharf as the red car roared after them. In the front seat, Tommo and Bazza grinned maliciously.

'You keep going,' Riana yelled. She tossed the spear to Josie, grabbed the bucket from Ben and ducked behind a pillar. Josie and Ben ran on. As the car bore down on them, Riana leaped from behind the pillar and hurled the bucket. Fish and murky seawater hit the windscreen, blocking Tommo's vision. The car swerved and crashed into a stack of cartons and rubbish bins.

For a moment, nothing happened, then there was a cry of rage from inside the car. The front passenger door flew open and Bazza leaped out. Riana took off along the pier. Bazza raced after her, leaving Tommo raging about the damage to his car.

Riana raced around a corner of the warehouse. Bazza followed, ready to pounce, but Josie stuck the spear between his feet and Bazza tripped. He sprawled face first onto the wooden decking.

'Come on,' Josie yelled.

Riana, Josie and Ben ran to the end of the pier and onto the street. Behind them, Tommo's car squealed to a halt beside Bazza. Still groggy, he staggered to his feet and jumped in. Smoke poured from the back wheels as the car roared on.

'I thought you were going fishing?' Brian said as he and Paul came out of their front door. Paul was carrying a bulging overnight bag. 'Looks like you're moving out.'

'I just brought a change of clothes in case the weather turns bad,' Paul said quickly. Riana's clothes were hidden in the bag under his. 'Dad, can I have some money? I'll need to get lunch and I might have to buy bait or something. Twenty should do it.'

Brian took out his wallet and handed Paul a note.

'Thanks. Well, I'd better be going.'

Brian put a hand on his shoulder. 'Hop in the car. I'll drop you at Alex's.'

'I don't mind walking,' Paul said.

'Don't be silly. It's about time I met Alex's father.'

As Brian went towards the car, Paul desperately tried to think of a way to keep him away from Alex's father. 'Look,' he cried. 'Here comes Gina.'

Brian turned and saw their attractive young housekeeper walking towards them. She waved. Brian blushed. 'Does she really think I'm ... you know ... a ...,' he whispered nervously to Paul.

'A spunk? Yeah. Go on. Talk to her.' Paul pushed his father towards Gina.

'What about?'

'Anything.'

'Morning, Mr Reynolds,' Gina called.

Brian smiled nervously. 'I'm ... er ... I'll get the door.' He hurried towards the front door and opened it.

'Don't worry, Dad,' Paul said, smiling. 'I'll

walk.'

Alex was waiting impatiently outside his garage as Paul came up the street lugging the overnight bag.

'Got the tickets?' Paul asked.

Alex held out four train tickets. 'Got the money?'

Paul took out the twenty dollars his father had given him. Alex took the money and put it with the tickets in his wallet. 'What about Katrina?'

'I called her. She's meeting us at the harbour. Come on.'

Alex shouldered the garbage bag containing the power suit and they hurried away.

'I think we've lost them,' Josie panted, looking back along the narrow street. She, Riana and Ben slowed to a walk.

'Let's go back to the warehouse,' Riana said. 'Paul will be there soon.'

There was a screech of tyres as the red car roared into the street behind them.

'This way,' Josie shouted and led them into a side-street. It was a dead end.

'We're trapped,' Riana cried.

Josie quickly looked around. The front door of a nearby house was open. 'No we're not!'

Josie, Riana and Ben jumped the garden wall and raced inside the house.

A young couple, still in their dressing-gowns, looked up from their breakfast croissants as the three kids ran into the kitchen.

'Hi,' Josie called as she pushed past the stunned couple.

'Sorry,' Riana added.

'Bye,' Ben said.

'Do something,' the woman cried to her husband as the kids ran out the back door. 'Assert yourself.'

The man went to the door and saw Riana, Josie and Ben scrambling over the fence.

'Stop,' he yelled. They ignored him and disappeared.

'That was assertive?' the woman asked sarcastically. She turned at the sound of heavy footsteps coming along the corridor. 'I'll handle it this time.'

Bazza and Tommo lumbered into the kitchen. They both looked mean and Bazza's cheek was bleeding from his fall. The woman backed nervously away.

'Now look here, lads,' the man said in a school-teacher's voice. 'This is just not on ... '

'Where are they?' Bazza snarled. The couple pointed at the back door. Bazza and Tommo raced out.

'Don't just stand there,' the woman whimpered, 'call the police.'

Paul and Alex sauntered along the street towards the pier. For the first time in days, Paul felt relaxed. Ashka was defeated and Riana could go safely home.

'You kids are dogmeat,' an angry voice yelled.

Paul looked up. All his good feelings vanished when he saw Bazza and Tommo chasing Riana, Josie and Ben into the warehouse. By the time Paul and Alex reached the door it had been secured from the inside.

'There must be another way in,' Paul said. They hurried around the side of the building and found a broken window. As Alex squeezed

through the narrow opening, he lost his
footing on the sill and tumbled into the dark
interior. Paul peered through the broken glass.
'Are you OK?'

Alex got to his feet, brushing himself down.
'Yeah. Give me the suit.' He didn't notice his
wallet lying on the floor.

Paul handed the power suit through the
window, then climbed in. They heard the
sound of angry voices and hurried through the
gloomy building.

Riana, Josie and Ben were struggling to hold
a sheet of corrugated iron across the doorway
to their room as Tommo savagely kicked it
from the other side. 'You kids are stuffed,' he
yelled. 'There's no way out!'

Tommo gave the barricade another kick but
it held firm. He saw a heavy timber beam lying
against the wall. 'Grab that,' he said to Bazza.
'We'll break it down.'

Paul and Alex peeked around a corner and
watched as Tommo and Bazza started to ram
the barricade with the beam.

'Give me the power suit,' Paul whispered to

Alex.

As he started to put it on, the battering ram brought the barricade down and Tommo and Bazza charged into the room.

'Rack off, creeps,' Josie screeched, pushing Ben behind her.

'Last night you made me look like an idiot,' Tommo said menacingly. 'Today you damage my car. Now you're gonna pay.'

Ben whimpered. Riana picked up an old rubbish bin lid to defend herself but Tommo lashed out with a karate kick and the lid flew from Riana's hands.

'Hurry up!' Alex said to Paul, who was struggling with the power suit buckles.

'I am. Distract them or something.'

Alex gathered his courage and then hurried to the doorway and knocked. The youths whirled around.

'Excuse me,' Alex said politely. 'I'm from the Young Friendly Association. We're opening a new activity centre for homeless youth. Would either of you be interested in joining?'

'Take a hike, snot features,' Bazza growled.

'We've got a pingpong table and three chess sets.'

Tommo pulled Alex into the room and pushed him against a wall. 'Do you have any punching bags?'

Alex shook his head.

'How would you like to become one?' Tommo asked, raising his fist.

'Paul,' Alex wailed.

'Leave him alone.'

The youths looked round and saw Paul coming through the door. Sunlight glinted off the copper fittings on the power suit.

'And who do you think you are?' Bazza sneered. 'Roboflop?' Tommo and Bazza guffawed.

'You'd better leave now or you're in big trouble,' Alex warned as he dodged away from Tommo.

'Really?' Tommo sneered.

Paul struck his wrists together and energised the suit. The youths gaped as a power-bolt flew from Paul's hand and hit the ceiling above their heads. An avalanche of dust, dirt and bird droppings crashed down on them.

'Want some more?' Paul yelled.

Sneezing and coughing, Bazza and Tommo

stumbled out of the room and ran from the warehouse.

'What is that thing?' Ben asked, staring in awe at Paul.

'A power suit,' Riana told him. 'It's from my world.'

They heard the sound of an approaching police siren.

'It's the cops,' Alex yelled. 'Let's vamoose!'

Ben grabbed Josie's hand and tried to pull her towards the door but she didn't move.

'We can't live like this any more, Ben,' she said gently. 'It's time we turned ourselves in.' She turned to Riana. 'Wherever it is, I hope you get home.'

Riana hugged Josie. Behind them, a man in a suit stepped through the doorway.

'Are you a detective?' Ben asked anxiously.

The man chuckled. 'No, I'm an accountant. I'm looking for a girl called Josie.'

Josie stepped cautiously forward. 'That's me.'

'I got your note,' the man said. 'It was a bit of a surprise.'

Josie stared at him. 'Are you Peter Eriksen?'

The man nodded. Father and daughter looked at each other nervously.

'I can see your mother in you,' Peter said, smiling.

Josie put her arm around Ben. 'This is my half-brother, Ben.'

'Pleased to meet you, Ben.' Peter held out his hand and Ben shook it warily.

'Are we coming to live with you?' Ben asked.

'We'll see,' Peter replied. 'We've got a lot to talk about.'

The police siren stopped outside the warehouse.

'Look, this is really touching and all,' Alex said quickly, 'but we'd better get out of here.'

'Wait!' Ben held out his Gameboy to Riana. 'You were just starting to get good. Take it back with you.'

Riana took the toy and hugged Ben.

'Thanks for everything, Riana,' Josie said.

With a farewell wave, Paul, Alex and Riana hurried towards the back of the warehouse.

Two policemen came to the front door of the warehouse as Josie, Ben and Peter emerged.

'Morning, officers,' Peter said cheerily. 'I saw some kids running out of here and thought I'd better have a look. The place seems empty now.'

One of the policemen stared at Josie and Ben. 'Who are these two?'

'My children,' Peter answered. 'Come on, kids, get in the car.'

Ben smiled at Josie. She smiled back and took his hand. Together they walked towards her father's car.

'Slow down,' Alex cried as he followed Paul and Riana towards the railway station. 'The train doesn't go for twenty minutes.'

'Isn't Katrina coming?' Riana asked Paul.

'She was supposed to meet us. She's going to be really upset she missed out on this.'

'Yeah,' Alex said. 'Her folks still think she's nuts. I wonder if I can get a refund on her ticket.' He reached into his pocket to get his wallet but his hand came out empty. 'My wallet's gone! The tickets were in it.'

The two policemen moved carefully through the derelict warehouse.

'This place should be boarded up,' one said as a rotted floorboard cracked under his foot. 'It's a deathtrap.'

He saw something on the floor by the window. It was Alex's wallet.

As the policeman picked up the wallet, Katrina ran through the door, carrying a camera. 'Paul?' she called. 'Riana?'

Katrina stared in dismay at the policemen.

Paul and Riana followed Alex along the street towards his house. He stopped outside a neighbour's front gate. 'You guys wait here. I'll scam some money off Nick and we can catch the next train.'

As Alex approached his house, he saw a police car parked in the driveway. A policeman was talking to his father. Mr Katsonis saw Alex and pointed. Alex quickly motioned for Paul and Riana to stay out of sight, then walked nonchalantly up to his father. 'Hi, Pop. What's happening?'

The policeman held up Alex's wallet. 'I found this in an old building by the harbour this morning.'

'Thanks,' Alex said, reaching for the wallet. His father grabbed it first.

'You were supposed to have gone fishing with Paul and his father,' Mr Katsonis said angrily. 'What's going on?'

'I ... um,' Alex stammered.

'What were you doing in that building?' the policeman inquired.

Behind his back, Alex signalled to Paul and Riana. They hurried back up the street as Mr Katsonis dragged a protesting Alex towards the front door.

Christine looked up from her sketchpad as Gina came into the kitchen with the vacuum cleaner.

'How come you haven't got a boyfriend?' Christine asked.

'I don't know,' Gina replied, checking the spaghetti sauce that was bubbling on the stove. 'I guess the boys I meet aren't smart enough to appreciate me.'

'My dad's really smart. He's a scientist. Do you think he's handsome?'

Gina smiled as she plugged in the vacuum

cleaner. 'He's the most handsome scientist I know.'

Christine smiled back as she imagined her father's and Gina's wedding. A pebble hit the window next to her. Christine looked out and was surprised to see Paul crouched beside the big rubbish bin in the back garden. He put his finger over his lips and beckoned to her.

'What are you doing here?' Christine asked as she came out.

Riana stepped from behind the bin. 'Alex lost the train tickets,' she explained. 'We need money to buy some more.'

'I haven't got any,' Christine said.

'What about your piggy bank?' Paul asked.

'That's for Christmas!'

'I'll pay you back,' Paul promised. 'It's for Riana. Please?'

Christine nodded and went back into the house. A few minutes later, the back door opened and Gina came out, carrying the dust-bag from the vacuum cleaner. She headed towards the bin where Paul and Riana were

hiding.

'Gina,' Christine called from the back door. 'I think the spaghetti sauce is burning. I'll empty that.' She took the dust-bag and Gina hurried back inside.

Christine took her piggy bank from under her jumper and gave it to Paul.

'Thanks, Chris.' Paul turned to Riana. 'Let's go.'

'Riana, wait.' Christine took off her silver neck chain and put it around Riana's neck. 'Now you'll always remember me.'

Riana hugged Christine, then she and Paul ran to the back fence and climbed over.

'The sauce was fine,' Gina called from the back door.

Christine smiled. 'Good.'

Paul and Riana found it hard to talk on the train journey up to the cave. Goodbyes were hard, especially when there was no chance they would ever see each other again. They trudged through the countryside to the Mount Lara school camp and up the trail to the cave.

Paul found the cable which he had left

hanging from the tree beneath the power lines. He secured it to a rock in the cave mouth, then checked his watch. 'It's after midday. Ready?'

Riana came out of the bush, dressed once more in the clothes from her world. They looked at each other awkwardly. Then Paul turned away and switched on the two-way radio. There was the sound of static. He pressed the talk button.

Correon was waiting by the iron stand at the base of the Summoning Tower. Paul's voice came from the Eyestone in his hand. 'Correon, it's Paul. Are you there?'

'Yes, Paul,' the old Spellbinder said eagerly. 'Are you ready?'

'The cable's in place. Put in the Eyestone.'

Correon placed his Eyestone in the metal dish on the stand and moved back. Power crackled around the top of the Summoning Tower, and a bolt of energy flashed to the dish.

Hidden among the rocks, Ashka watched, fascinated, as the air behind the dish seemed to ripple.

Electricity leaped from the overhead power lines and surged down the cable. With a flash of light, the energy doorway opened.

Paul smiled at Riana. 'See? I said I'd find a way to get you home.' He held out the power suit. 'Take this back to Correon.'

'Why don't you give it to him yourself?' Riana asked. She grabbed Paul's hand and pulled him through the doorway.

Correon watched in amazement as Riana and Paul stepped through the doorway into the Spellbinders' world.

'I never thought I'd see you again,' Paul said, grinning at Correon. He held out the power suit.

'Thank you,' Correon said, taking it. 'And I

have something for you.' He handed Paul the video-camera.

'Now you can show my world to your father,' Riana said.

'And to Katrina's mum,' Paul added. 'Then she won't think Katrina's crazy any more.'

'Come on,' said Riana, 'I want to get home.'

Paul started to go back towards the doorway but Riana took his arm. 'You can't go yet. You have to come and say goodbye to my family. You can take their pictures.'

'We can't leave the doorway open,' Paul said. 'What if someone goes through?'

Correon removed the Eyestone from the dish and the energy doorway faded. 'Now you have to come.'

Paul grinned and the three headed down the trail towards Clayhill.

'Everything in Paul's world is bigger and faster and more powerful than here,' Riana told Correon along the way. 'But I got used to it. I even learnt to use a computer.'

'What is that?' Correon asked.

'It's like a box that can think,' Riana explained. 'They solve all your problems.'

'Not all of them,' Paul corrected. 'They can't help me get on better with my dad.' Riana laughed.

'Computers can do lots of different things,' Paul went on. 'Store knowledge, control machines, design new technologies ...' He saw that Correon did not understand. 'Take our flying ships. Now that they're computer-controlled, they can fly higher and faster than ever before.'

Creeping through the undergrowth above the trail, Ashka listened intently to the conversation. She wondered how she could make use of this extraordinary information.

Bron was on a ladder, hammering together the frame of his new cottage when Correon, Paul and Riana came into Clayhill. He leaped to the ground and ran to his daughter.

'I always knew you'd come back to us,' Bron cried with relief as he hugged her.

'I wasn't so sure,' a tearful Maran admitted as she hurried over with Arla and Jal. Riana opened her arms wide and embraced her family.

Bron and Maran suddenly remembered they were in the presence of a Spellbinder and bowed to Correon.

'Thank you for bringing our daughter back, Regent,' Bron said humbly.

'It wasn't me,' Correon said. 'It was Paul.'

'Thank you,' Maran said. To Paul's surprise, she kissed him.

'What happened to our house?' Riana asked, staring at the charred remains of the old cottage.

'Ashka burnt it,' Arla told her.

'Where is she now?' Paul asked, looking anxiously around.

'Ashka hasn't been seen since she escaped from the castle,' Correon replied. 'But you don't have to worry. Without a power suit, she's harmless.'

Correon noticed Gryvon skulking inside the frame of the cottage. Part of his punishment for conspiring with Ashka had been to help Bron rebuild the cottage.

'Gryvon,' the Spellbinder said sternly, 'do you have something to say?'

Gryvon came reluctantly out of the cottage

and faced Paul and Riana. 'Paul, Riana, I'd like
to apologise for everything I did to you.'

Paul nodded stiffly, but Riana turned away.
'Arla, Jal. I brought you a present from Paul's
world,' she said.

Riana pulled Ben's Gameboy from her
pocket and turned it on. The electronic beep
startled Jal. 'It's just a toy,' Riana reassured
him. 'I'll show you how it works.'

'I should be getting back,' Paul said.

Maran took his arm. 'You can't go yet. You
have to eat with us.'

Bron saw Gryvon staring at the Gameboy.
'Don't just stand there,' he snapped, 'go and
get some more poles.'

Gryvon stalked angrily across the village to
a stack of poles at the edge of the forest. As he
bent to pick one up, a low whistle came from
the trees. Gryvon looked up and was surprised
to see Ashka beckoning him. Checking that
no-one was watching, Gryvon ran to her.
Ashka pulled him out of sight behind a tree.

'The Spellbinders are still looking for you,'
Gryvon warned. 'If they catch you, you'll be
banished.'

'That's why I'm going to Paul's world.'

Gryvon stared at Ashka in disbelief.

'I know how to get there,' she said, 'but I need your help.'

'I can't,' Gryvon protested, 'I'm in enough trouble as it is.'

'Are you going to let those ignorant villagers treat you like a servant for the rest of your life?' Ashka sneered.

'Correon said there was a chance I could be an Apprentice again.'

'Forget Correon,' Ashka snapped. 'There is power in Paul's world that will make me invincible. When I come back, I'll have knowledge that will make the Spellbinders my servants.'

The remains of a hearty lunch lay on a table outside the partially built cottage. Bron was playing a merry tune on his mandolin. Correon had taken off his power suit and was dancing a jig with Maran. Paul couldn't help smiling as he filmed the celebration.

Riana left Jal and Arla playing with the Gameboy and went to Paul. 'My mother dancing with a Spellbinder,' she said in wonder. 'Who would have thought it?'

'Maybe things will be different here now,' Paul said.

'Fire,' Gryvon yelled. 'Fire!'

Everyone turned and saw Gryvon running towards them from the barn. Behind him, smoke billowed out of the door.

'Get buckets!' Bron shouted.

Villagers came running from everywhere. They formed a human chain from the stream to the barn and passed buckets of water along it to fight the blaze. Gryvon smiled. The diversion was working.

While all eyes were on the burning barn, Ashka sneaked out of the forest and hurried to Bron's cottage. The spare power suit was hanging on a beam next to Correon's. Ashka lifted it down and ran back into the trees.

The villagers soon had the fire under control. The Summoner loudly praised Gryvon for his quick-wittedness in raising the alarm. Unable to stand the look of smugness on Gryvon's face, Riana went to wash the soot from her face.

As she approached the stream, Riana saw something gleaming in the forest. Curious, she made her way into the trees. There was a rustle from behind a bush. Riana put down the bucket and went towards it. She pulled back the branches and was horrified to see Ashka, tightening the last buckle on her power suit.

Riana turned and ran but tripped over the bucket. She scrambled to her feet but Ashka stepped from behind the bush and energised the power suit.

'Don't make a sound,' Ashka hissed. 'Now move.'

Riana looked desperately towards the village but Ashka pushed her forward. As they moved through the forest, Riana pretended to stumble and fell against a tree. She quickly pulled the silver chain over her head and hung it on a low branch just before Ashka pushed her on.

'You won't get away with this,' Riana protested. 'Correon and the whole village will come looking for me.' She snapped a twig on a bush.

'Quiet,' Ashka ordered. They came to a fork

in the trail and Ashka pushed Riana towards one of the paths.

Again Riana pretended to stumble and fall. She grabbed a rock and quickly drew an arrow in the earth pointing along the track.

'That won't help you,' Ashka sneered, erasing the arrow with her foot. She pulled Riana to her feet and pushed her forward.

The track led to a rocky hill. Ashka pulled away a heap of branches at the base of the hill, revealing the narrow entrance to a cave. She pushed Riana inside.

Ashka lit a candle and Riana realised that the cave was Ashka's hideout. There was a rough bed of branches and leaves and the remains of a cooking fire.

'Now, tell me everything you know about Paul's world,' Ashka commanded.

'I don't know much,' Riana replied. 'I wasn't there long.'

'But you told Correon that everything is faster and more powerful.' Ashka smiled at Riana's shocked reaction. 'That's right. I've been following you ever since you arrived.'

'Paul's world is huge,' Riana explained,

173

trying to control her fear. 'I hardly saw any of it.'

'What about the thinking computers?' Ashka asked. 'How do they work?'

'That depends on what software you have.'

Ashka shook her head. 'I don't understand. What do computers look like? Do they have to be fed?'

Riana laughed. 'They're not alive.'

'Could I carry one?'

Riana suddenly understood what Ashka was planning. 'You can't go to Paul's world.'

Ashka smiled. 'Why not?'

Alien Invasion

'Paul! Bron!' Correon shouted.

Paul and Bron ran back to the cottage and found Correon buckling on his power suit. Gryvon was lurking by the table, hungrily eyeing the remains of lunch.

'Ashka's power suit is gone,' the worried Spellbinder told them.

'We can't find Riana,' Paul said.

'Perhaps she stole the power suit,' Gryvon suggested.

Paul turned angrily on the smirking youth. 'You're not an Apprentice anymore.' He took a step towards Gryvon, clenching his fists.

Bron held him back. 'No, Paul. He's not worth it. We have to find Riana.'

Paul glared at Gryvon, then followed Bron and Correon into the forest. Once they were gone, Gryvon crammed his mouth full of bread and cheese. He noticed the Gameboy lying on the table where Jal had dropped it. Checking that no-one was watching, he slid it into his pocket and hurried after Paul and the others.

'Here,' Bron called.

Pushing through the undergrowth, Paul and Correon found Bron holding up Riana's bucket. They looked at the ground for tracks, then Paul saw something glinting in a nearby tree.

'My sister gave this to Riana,' Paul said, lifting the thin silver chain off the branch.

'What was Riana doing out here?' Bron asked.

'Maybe she's following whoever stole the power suit,' Paul suggested.

Bron spotted the broken twig on the bush. 'She's left a trail,' he said, pointing to a track through the forest. 'This way.'

He dropped the bucket and ran along the track, following Riana's signs. Paul and Correon went after him. The signs stopped at a fork in the track.

'Which way?' Paul asked.

'We'll have to split up. I'll go this way. Yell if you find her.' Bron headed along the left fork.

Paul and Correon took the track to the right, unaware that Gryvon was shadowing them.

Riana squatted on the floor of the dim cave, watching Ashka pacing by the entrance.

'I don't understand,' Ashka said. 'Paul's father builds new things but he isn't a Spellbinder?'

'There aren't any Spellbinders in Paul's world.'

'Then who tells the people how to behave?'

'News-readers,' Riana lied.

'What are news-readers?'

'Little people who live in boxes in everyone's houses.'

'Extraordinary,' Ashka exclaimed. 'Do the news-readers punish people who won't do as they're told?'

'No, that's done by school teachers. They're terrifying. They make you play sport.' Riana had to work hard to keep a straight face as Ashka listened intently to every word.

'What is sport?'

'You have to run around a field as fast as you can while everyone tries to jump on you.'

'Paul's world sounds dangerous,' Ashka mused.

Riana got to her feet. 'It is. I don't think you should go there. I was lucky to get back here alive. I nearly got eaten by a car.' She edged towards the cave entrance.

'A car?'

'They're wild animals. They live in car parks. Sometimes they escape and run people down. I nearly got gored by a car horn ...'

'You're lying!' Ashka snapped. 'I saw cars on Paul's picture box. They're not animals.'

'Well, they're like animals. They've just got wheels instead of legs.'

Riana made a break for the entrance but Ashka grabbed her. 'Has everything you've told me been lies?'

Riana said nothing.

'We're going to Clayhill and you're going to lure Paul from the village,' Ashka told her. 'If I have him, his father will do whatever I ask.'

'Riana?' Paul's voice came from outside the cave.

Before Riana could yell for help, Ashka clamped her mouth shut.

Paul trotted along the track at the base of the cliff, searching for more of Riana's signs. 'Riana,' he called again.

'Hello, Paul.'

Paul turned and saw Ashka coming out of the cave, holding a struggling Riana in front of her.

'She's trying to get to your world,' Riana yelled.

'I'll let her go if you come with me,' Ashka said.

Paul imagined how helpless Ashka would be in a modern city. To Riana's dismay, he walked towards Ashka. She pushed Riana away and grabbed him.

'Let the boy go!' Correon roared.

Ashka whirled around as Correon appeared along the track. Paul twisted out of her grip and ran with Riana into the cave.

'Out of my way, old man,' Ashka snarled, energising her power suit. 'I've beaten you once in combat.'

'Only because you cheated.' Correon energised his own suit.

He raised his arm to hurl a bolt but Gryvon charged out of the trees and rammed him from behind. Correon fell forward and struck his head on the ground. He lay still.

'Get Paul,' Ashka cried.

Gryvon ran towards the cave but a rock flew out of the darkness, narrowly missing his head. Gryvon ducked back against the cliff as another rock flew past.

'Paul! Correon!' Bron called from the forest.

'Da!' Riana yelled from the cave. 'Help. It's Ashka.'

Seething with frustration, Ashka ran for the trees. Gryvon raced after her.

Paul and Riana emerged from the cave and hurried to Correon. Paul helped him sit up and the old Spellbinder opened his eyes. 'What happened?'

'Ashka is trying to get to Paul's world,' Riana explained.

Correon struggled to his feet. 'We must get to the Summoning Tower first.'

Ashka and Gryvon hurried up the steep track and stopped at the edge of the clearing. The area around the Summoning Tower was deserted.

'Watch carefully,' Ashka said, as she went to the base of the tower. She took the Eyestone from her power suit and placed it in the metal dish on the stand. Power began to crackle around the tower and along the cables to the dish. There was a flash of energy and Gryvon stared in amazement as the doorway to Paul's world opened.

'When I've gone, take the Eyestone with you,' Ashka said. 'Come back every day at dawn and open the doorway. I'm relying on you, Gryvon. You're the only way I can get back.'

Gryvon nodded. 'I won't let you down.'

Ashka moved warily towards the doorway and reached out. Her hand disappeared through the rippling curtain of energy. Ashka took a step forward and vanished.

Ashka stepped out of the doorway, ready to energise her power suit. This was a new world. She had no idea what threats could be lurking nearby; there could be school teachers hidden amongst the trees. Ashka looked up and saw a metal cable above her head. Power crackled between it and the doorway.

'Take the Eyestone from the stand,' Ashka called through the doorway.

Gryvon quickly did as he was told. Power stopped crackling along the cable and the doorway faded.

Ashka quickly climbed the rocky slope beside the cave to survey the area for danger. She clambered onto a boulder high above the cave and gasped in amazement. Before her was a panoramic view of the ouskirts of Sydney. Buildings and roads stretched as far as the eye could see. Ashka was astounded. Paul's world was bigger than she had ever imagined.

Paul moved warily into the deserted clearing beneath the Summoning Tower. 'Looks like we beat Ashka here.'

'You must go back now,' Correon said.

'But I left the video-camera back at Clayhill.'

'There's no time to get it.'

Correon took the Eyestone from his power suit and placed it in the dish on the stand. Energy crackled around the tower and there was a flash as the doorway opened. Correon stared at the rippling energy. 'Before I met you,' he told Paul, 'I thought I knew everything.'

'You can never know everything.'

'I certainly hope not. Then there would be nothing to learn.'

The old Spellbinder smiled and held out his hand. Paul clasped it.

'I'll never see you again, will I?' Riana said.

Paul shook his head. Lost for words, he took Christine's chain from his pocket and hung it around Riana's neck. She hugged him tightly, then pushed him towards the doorway. 'Go home.'

Paul gave Riana and Correon a final wave and stepped through the doorway.

Paul emerged into the bright sunlight of his own world. He looked back through the doorway and saw Correon lift the Eyestone from the dish. The doorway faded and disappeared. Paul removed the cable from the cave mouth and then climbed the tree to unknot the other end of it, which was tied around a branch. However, the power flow had fused the knot solid, so he just coiled the cable up at the base of the tree.

Paul went to the cave mouth and disconnected the radio equipment that Alex and Katrina had set up. He stowed it in his bag and took a final look around before heading down the trail towards the school camp. Now the adventure was over and his life could go back to normal.

Ashka dragged her eyes away from the breathtaking view and looked down. The cable had gone! She scanned the clearing and saw Paul disappearing down the trail. Furious with herself for becoming distracted, she scrambled down the hillside after him.

Paul trudged along the dirt road away from the school camp. He reached the intersection with the highway and started the long walk to the railway station. An old green Morris pulled up beside him and an elderly nun rolled down the window. 'What are you doing all the way out here?'

'I've been at the school camp and got left behind,' Paul said, feeling a bit uncomfortable at the lie. 'Could you give me a lift to the station?'

'The camp's been empty for a week,' the nun said. 'If you're going to tell stories, at least try being a little more inventive. The last two kids I gave a lift to said they were rescuing a friend trapped in a parallel world. Now that's what I call a story.' Paul realised she must be talking about Alex and Katrina. The nun laughed at his stunned expression. 'Hop in.'

Ashka came running up the dirt road and saw Paul getting into the car. By the time she reached the highway, the car had driven off. Ashka let out a cry of frustration and started hurrying after it along the centre of the road.

A raucous noise made Ashka turn. She saw a large vehicle bearing down on her. Its horn blared again. Ashka quickly energised her power suit and hurled a power-bolt. It hit the road in front of the truck, showering it with sparks. The truck swerved past Ashka and ran off the road.

Ashka ran over and wrenched the door open. Greg, the young driver, stared at her in terror. 'What do you want?'

Ashka got into the cab. 'There's a boy ahead of us. I must catch him. You will take me.'

Greg cowered against his door, staring at Ashka's power suit. 'You're an alien, aren't you?'

'A what?'

'You're not going to take over my body or suck out my brains, are you?'

'Go!' Ashka ordered.

Greg quickly started the engine and drove away.

A train was waiting as the nun's car pulled up outside the station. Paul leaped out. 'Thanks for the lift, Sister Josephine.'

The nun waved as Paul hurried towards the station. Behind them, Greg's truck came hurtling into the town.

'There he is,' Ashka cried. 'Stop!'

Greg jammed on the brakes and the truck screeched to a halt. Ashka threw the door open.

'What do you want a boy for?' Greg quickly asked. 'Take me. I'm a terrific specimen of humanity. I'd be happy to breed with your race.'

'If you tell anyone about me,' Ashka said menacingly, 'I *will* come back and suck your brains out.'

Greg gulped. Ashka got out and ran into the station. She reached the platform just as the train was pulling out. There was no sign of Paul.

'You!' she called to the station attendant. 'Where's that ... thing going?'

'The city. There's another one at six.'

Ashka ran out of the station and saw Greg's truck disappearing into the distance. She snarled in frustration. Then a powerful throbbing sound attracted her attention. A three-wheeled vehicle was roaring towards her, ridden by a large man wearing a black helmet and black leather clothes. Ashka stepped onto the road and held up her hand. The three-wheeled motorcycle skidded to a halt in front of her.

'What do you think you're doing?' the rider yelled.

'What is that?' Ashka asked, pointing at the gleaming, black and chrome motorcycle.

'A Harley trike. Best bike in the world. Finest chick magnet money can buy.'

'I want a ride.'

The rider grinned at Ashka. 'Of course you do.' He tossed her a spare helmet. 'I'm Chopper. Hop on. Where do you want to go?'

'The city,' Ashka replied, climbing on behind him.

'Anywhere particular? I know some good pubs.'

'I need to find a boy called Paul.'

'Paul who?'

'Paul whose father is the scientist.'

'My dad's a pest exterminator. Won't I do?'

Chopper laughed, then turned the ignition key. The bike roared into life. Chopper twisted the handgrip and Ashka was nearly thrown off as the powerful machine accelerated away.

Christine sat at the kitchen table while Gina carefully applied a final touch of mascara to her eyelashes and then held up the mirror. Christine liked the effect. It made her look a lot older than ten.

'You like kids, don't you?' Christine asked.

'Yeah. One day, I'm going to get married and have a really big family.' Gina began putting her makeup away.

'I'd like to live in a big family,' Christine said wistfully. Gina smiled.

Paul came in through the back door, carrying his overnight bag and a plastic shopping bag.

'How did it go?' Christine asked, winking at her brother.

'Everything went according to plan,' Paul answered.

Brian came into the kitchen. 'How was the fishing trip?'

'Great. I caught these.' He opened the shopping bag and displayed four fresh trout. 'We could have them for dinner.'

'They're trout,' Brian said, puzzled. 'They're freshwater fish. I thought you went sea fishing?'

'Well ... ah ... the truth is, I didn't actually catch any fish,' Paul confessed. 'So I bought some. I didn't want to come home empty-handed.'

'Seeing as there're four, can Gina stay for dinner?' Christine asked.

'I'm sure Gina has other plans,' Brian said.

'As it happens, I haven't. I'd love to stay, Mr Reynolds. And I know a terrific recipe for trout.'

'Please, call me Brian.'

Gina smiled at him. Christine nudged Paul.

Sitting on the back of the three-wheeled motorcycle, Ashka looked up in awe at the towering buildings as Chopper cruised along the street. It was night and the city was alive with lights and people. Chopper pulled over to the side of the road.

'Keep going, Chopper,' Ashka said.

'What's the point? It's a million to one chance that we'll run into this Paul just by riding around. I need a drink.' He got off the bike and headed towards a pub.

Ashka slid forward on the seat and grabbed the handlebars. 'Give me the keys,' she called.

Chopper laughed. 'No way.'

Anger flared in Ashka's eyes. 'Do as I say!'

'I don't take orders from a chick!' Chopper snapped.

Ashka energised her power suit and hurled a power-bolt at the rubbish bin beside him. It exploded into flames. Chopper quickly tossed her the keys. Recalling what Chopper had done, Ashka started the bike, put it in gear and twisted the throttle. A car screeched to a halt as Ashka roared away from the kerb without even looking.

'My bike!' Chopper wailed, tears welling in his eyes.

'This is really good, Gina,' Christine said, taking another mouthful of Mediterranean baked trout. Brian and Paul nodded their agreement. Gina smiled proudly.

'Dad, can you and I go fishing some time?' Paul asked.

'Girls can fish,' Christine protested. 'I want to come too.'

'Yes, Christine,' Brian said. 'We can all go.'

'And Gina?'

Gina shook her head. 'I'm not really into catching fish. I feel sorry for the worms. If I was lost in the bush, I'd never survive. Paul, I've been meaning to ask you. What was it like when you were lost?'

Paul stopped with his fork midway to his mouth. Brian looked warily at him, waiting for the explosion of anger.

'Well, it wasn't easy,' Paul began, putting down his fork. 'The hardest thing was to keep from panicking.'

Brian breathed a sigh of relief.

'I'd never cope if something like that happened to me,' Gina said. 'If I can't start the day without a hot shower and a strong black coffee, I'm hopeless.'

'I like to jog in the mornings,' Brian said to divert the conversation. 'When I've got the time.'

Gina shuddered. 'I hate jogging. But I like to dance. Sometimes I go to a club and dance till dawn.'

'Dad likes to dance,' Christine said enthusiastically.

Paul laughed. 'No he doesn't. He's hopeless.'

'I wouldn't say hopeless,' Brian said indignantly.

'You wouldn't, but Mum did.'

There was a silence as the Reynoldses remembered the missing member of their family.

'Who wants some dessert?' Gina said brightly. 'I make an excellent apple crumble.' She got up and started to clear the plates.

'We'll do that. Won't we, Paul?' Christine pushed Gina back into her seat, then she and Paul cleared the plates and carried them into the kitchen.

'That's the first time Paul's talked about being lost without it turning into world war three,' Brian told Gina. 'You're a good influence on him.'

'He's a good kid. They both are. You must be an OK parent.'

Gina smiled again at Brian. He smiled back. Christine watched from the kitchen doorway, grinning.

Ashka pulled the bike into the kerb and groaned. She was exhausted from looking for

Paul, keeping control of the powerful machine and avoiding the other vehicles on the road. A tantalising smell reminded her that she was ravenous. She saw a man in a white apron by a cart hand something to a boy. He took a bite from it and walked away, chewing. Ashka grabbed the boy as he passed and pointed to the object in his hand. 'What is that?' she demanded.

'A hot dog,' the boy replied nervously.

Ashka let him go and rode the bike over the kerb. People scrambled out of her way as she rode along the pavement. The man behind the cart stared in amazement as she stopped in front of him. 'Give me a hot dog,' she ordered.

The man quickly prepared one and held it out. 'That'll be three fifty.'

'Three fifty what?'

'Don't get smart, lady. Just give me the money.'

'What is money?'

The man held up a ten-dollar note. Ashka snatched the note and examined it.

'Give that back!' The man made a grab for

the money but Ashka pushed him away. He staggered backwards into the cart, tipping it over. Hot water, sausages and tomato sauce bottles spilled over the pavement.

'Help! Police!' the man yelled. 'I'm being robbed.'

Ashka roared off down the pavement.

Ashka rode the bike along a deserted road beside a disused oil refinery. It was raining and she was cold and desperate to find shelter. As Ashka stared curiously at the maze of pipes and gantries inside the refinery, she noticed firelight flickering in the window of a corrugated iron shed. She rode the bike through the gates.

Ashka parked the bike by the shed and strode through the door. A man in a torn and filthy overcoat was heating a can of stew over a small fire on the floor.

'Wet night, eh?' the tramp said. 'Come in and dry off.'

Ashka went to the fire and warmed her hands over it. She watched hungrily as the tramp lifted the can from the flames and dug in with a spoon.

'Sorry,' he said, 'I'd share this with you but it's all I've got.'

'Then leave it and get out!'

'Listen, lady,' the tramp protested, 'I found this place.'

Ashka energised her power suit. The tramp stared as a ball of energy appeared in her hand. He dropped the can and fled out of the door. Ashka picked it up and sat by the fire. She wiped the spoon clean and began to eat.

Paul kicked the soccer ball towards the goal chalked on Alex's garage doors. Alex intercepted the ball and kicked it back. It soared over Paul's head, right into the hands of Katrina, who was coming up the street. She glared accusingly at the boys.

'Where were you yesterday? I went to the warehouse like you said but the police were there. They drove me home and Mum and Dad had a fit.'

'Chill out, Katrina.' Alex said. 'I got in trouble with the cops too.'

'We couldn't wait,' Paul explained. 'We had to get Riana back.'

'But you promised I could go to Riana's world! I had a camera and everything.'

'I didn't get to go either,' Alex grumbled.

'Did you bring back something to show my parents?' Katrina asked Paul.

'Well, I shot all this video footage of Riana's village ... but I had to leave the camera behind.'

'What?' Katrina screeched. 'Then you'll have to go back and get it.'

'The doorway stays closed,' Paul said firmly. 'I'm sorry. We all have to forget about the Spellbinders.'

'That's easy for you. You're not grounded for the rest of your life.' Katrina kicked the ball hard. It flew over the garage and into Alex's backyard. There was a crash of breaking glass.

'Alex!' Mr Katsonis bellowed.

In the city, Ashka trudged along the seemingly endless streets, beginning to doubt she would ever find Paul. She walked out of a laneway and into another street filled with cars and people hurrying in and out of shops.

'Great outfit!' a teenage girl said, staring in

admiration at Ashka's black leather power suit.

Her friend nodded. 'Real cyberpunk. Did you make it yourself?' She ran her hand over the copper fittings.

'I need information,' Ashka said. 'Who's in charge of this world?'

'What do you mean?' the girl asked.

'Who tells you what to do?'

'My boyfriend tried, so I dumped him,' she said. Her friend laughed.

'Quiet!' Ashka hissed. 'How do you learn about things?'

'Mostly from TV,' one answered.

'TV? Is that the box the news-reader lives in?' The girls looked at Ashka as if she was crazy, then nodded. 'Where do I find TV?'

The girls pointed across the road to a display of TV sets outside a shop. While Ashka's back was turned, the girls fled. Ashka crossed the street and warily entered the store.

The back wall was completely covered by television sets. Ashka went over and carefully ran her fingers over the picture on one of the screens.

'They're the very latest technology, madam,'

a salesman said. 'Flat screen, stereo, cable-ready ...'

'How do the news-readers fit in there?' Ashka asked. The salesman gaped as Ashka put her head behind the set and tried to look inside.

At the service desk, a customer was getting out his wallet. Ashka watched curiously as a shop assistant took his money and handed over a portable TV. The assistant put the money in the cash register.

'Now I understand!' Ashka took the ten-dollar note from her pocket. 'You swap this ... money for things you want.' She held out the note to the salesman. 'I want a TV.'

He laughed. 'I'm afraid that's not quite enough.'

'Where do I get more?'

'I think it's time madam was leaving.' The salesman took Ashka's arm and tried to lead her towards the door. Angry, Ashka threw him off and energised her power suit.

Immediately, everything electrical in the store went wild. Television screens fuzzed out, stereos blared music, the burglar alarm went off and the cash-register drawer sprang open. The shop assistant cowered in terror as Ashka cleared the register of bank notes and ran out of the shop. The salesman recovered his wits and raced after her yelling, 'Stop, thief!'

Ashka energised her power suit again. Cars stopped on the street and their alarms went off as the suit's magnetic field disrupted their electrical systems. Ashka hurled a power-bolt and the salesman dived onto the pavement. The glowing ball of energy flew over him and struck the display outside the shop. Six television sets exploded, showering the pavement with glass. Stunned pedestrians gaped as Ashka strode between the stalled cars and disappeared down the laneway.

Brian was humming merrily as he poured batter into a frying pan. The smell of cooking pancakes filled the kitchen.

'You haven't made these for breakfast for ages,' Paul said through a mouthful. 'What's the occasion?'

'No occasion. I just feel good.'

'Why?' Christine asked.

'Does there have to be a reason to feel good? The weather's fine, I've got two wonderful children.'

Christine winked at Paul. 'Dad, what do you think of Gina?'

'She cooks a great trout.' He took a sip from a mug of coffee.

'Are you going to marry her?'

Brian spluttered out his coffee. 'Christine, asking a woman to share your fish is a long way from asking her to share the rest of your life.' He quickly picked up the morning paper and started to read the front page.

'He didn't say no,' Christine whispered to Paul.

Brian laughed.

'What's funny?' Paul asked.

Brian read from the paper. ' "On Saturday a young farmer from Mount Lara claimed he was abducted by a beautiful alien woman wearing an electrically charged space suit ..." ' He stopped when he saw the look of horror on Paul's face. 'What's wrong?'

'Nothing, Dad,' Paul said quickly. 'Keep reading.'

'"Yesterday a woman wearing a similar suit caused thousands of dollars of damage in an electrical retail store ..."' Brian shook his head. 'Aliens on the front page. Must be a slow news day.' The phone rang. 'That'll be for me.'

As soon as Brian left the kitchen, Paul grabbed the newspaper and quickly scanned the article.

'What's wrong?' Christine asked.

Paul looked at Christine with fear in his eyes. 'I think Ashka's here.'

The Hunt for Ashka

It was Monday morning and Nathan was waiting eagerly by the school gate as Alex approached.

'Sorry, mate,' Alex said dejectedly, 'it's over between me and Katrina so I won't be needing these anymore.' He handed the borrowed two-way radio equipment back to the disappointed boy.

'What about the tapes?' Nathan asked.

'The tapes?'

'You promised to tape what you and Katrina said to each other. It was going to be the basis for my first novel.'

'Oh, right, those tapes,' Alex said, remembering the deal he'd made with Nathan to get the radio equipment from his father's shop. Alex sniggered. 'They were hot.'

Nathan's eyes widened in anticipation. **203**

'Excellent. Where are they?'

'Katrina burnt them in a fit of mad passion,' Alex lied. 'Sorry, man.'

Nathan was devastated. He'd already worked out how he was going to spend the first royalty cheque from his best-selling teenage romance novel.

Paul hurried across the yard and thrust a newspaper in Alex's face. 'Have you seen this?'

Alex read the article. 'Wow! A beautiful alien woman stalking the city. She must have come for my body.'

Paul pulled him away from Nathan. 'She's not an alien. I think it's Ashka!'

'The Spellbinder? Why would she come here?'

'She was banished. But she stole a power suit. Ashka's dangerous, Alex. We've got to find out what she's up to.'

'How are we going to find her?'

'I don't know.'

Outside the gate, Katrina got out of her mother's car.

'Hey!' Paul yelled but Katrina ignored him.

'It must be really hard having to see her

every day,' Nathan said to Alex.

'It's like a dagger piercing my heart,' Alex said, clutching his chest melodramatically.

'What are you talking about?' Paul asked.

'Haven't you heard?' Nathan said. 'Alex busted up with Katrina.'

Paul stared at Alex. 'But you and Katrina never ...'

'See you, Nathan.' Alex dragged Paul away.

The science laboratory was filling with students as Paul and Alex came in. Paul spotted Katrina sitting with her friend Lisa and went over to her.

'Listen,' he began, 'I'm really sorry about what happened with ...'

'I'm not talking to you,' Katrina snapped.

'But something weird's happened.'

'OK, settle down.' Ms Gibson stared at Paul. He left Katrina and sat next to Alex.

'Alan had a problem this morning that the rest of us can learn from,' Ms Gibson said. 'Alan?'

Looking uncomfortable, Smithy rose from his seat and held up a computer disk. 'I didn't want to forget my homework so I stuck my disk on the refrigerator with a magnet. Now it's all scrambled.'

The class groaned at his foolishness. Smithy sat down, his cheeks burning with embarrassment.

'It's not just magnets that can affect a computer disk,' Ms Gibson warned the class. 'Anything that produces an electro-magnetic field can do it. TVs, mobile phones, power lines ...'

Lisa stuck up her hand. 'Miss, is it true that living near power lines is dangerous?'

'There's evidence to suggest that, yes.'

An idea started to form in Paul's mind. 'How do you detect an electro-magnetic field?' he asked.

'With an instrument called a magnetometer.'

'Could we build one?'

'I suppose so. Why?'

'We could measure the level of electro-magnetic radiation around the school. Alex and I could do it as a special project.'

Alex glared at Paul.

'Good idea,' Ms Gibson said. 'If you see me at lunchtime, I'll help you with the equipment. Alright, open your textbooks at page 58.'

'What are you doing?' Alex whispered to Paul. 'I need extra work like I need a hole in the head.'

'Ashka's power suit is electro-magnetic,' Paul explained excitedly. 'If we build a magnetometer, the next time she uses it, we might be able to trace her.'

The boys grinned at each other. Across the classroom, Katrina watched them suspiciously.

Following Ms Gibson's instructions, Paul and Alex assembled a magnetometer in the science lab. It was a black box housing a battery-powered meter which measured magnetic field strength. Connected to the box by a short lead was a plastic sphere containing a coil of wire.

'When the coil detects a magnetic field, the meter will beep,' Paul explained. 'Then you move the coil around until the needle on the meter gives the highest reading. That gives us the direction. Get the magnet and we'll try it out.'

Alex put a large magnet on the bench.

'What are you two up to?' Katrina asked from the doorway.

Relieved that she was talking to him again, Paul got the newspaper out of his bag and pointed to the article. 'I think Ashka's in our world. We've built this to track her down.'

Paul moved the sphere towards the magnet and flicked the switch on the box. Nothing happened.

'What's wrong with it?' Alex asked.

'I don't know.' Paul checked the connections, then turned the switch off and on again. Still nothing happened.

'Let me have a look.' Katrina opened the back of the box and laughed. 'You boys think you're so clever.'

'We are,' said Alex. 'Usually.'

'Not this time. You've put the batteries in the wrong way.' Katrina reversed the batteries in their slots and closed the box. She held the magnet in front of the sphere and flicked the switch. The magnetometer started beeping and the needle moved to the far end of the dial.

'If we had two of these,' Katrina suggested, 'we could triangulate Ashka's signal.' Alex looked puzzled. 'Get a bearing on the signal from two directions,' she explained.

'Does this mean you're going to help?' Paul asked eagerly.

Paul, Alex and Katrina came out of the school, carrying two magnetometers and maps of Sydney.

'We'll split up,' Paul said. 'When you get a reading, mark the direction on the map. We'll meet back at Alex's in a couple of hours and compare results.'

'I wish you still had those radios,' Katrina said to Alex. 'Then when we get a reading, we could triangulate right away.'

Alex saw Nathan watching from across the yard. 'Kiss me,' he said to Katrina. 'Quick.'

'In your dreams!'

'Just a little one. For Nathan.'

Katrina saw Nathan watching and got the message. She kissed Alex lightly on the lips. **209**

'Katrina!'

Katrina turned in dismay and saw her mother standing by the gate. She was furious. 'Get in the car!'

Katrina hurried over to her. 'Mum, this isn't what you think. It's a science project.'

'I can't trust you out of my sight for a second, can I?'

'But, Mum.'

'I haven't got time to argue,' Mrs Muggleton snapped. 'I've got a hairdressing appointment in town.'

'I've got homework to do,' Katrina protested.

'I'll drop you at the library. You can do your homework there.'

Katrina gave Paul and Alex a despairing look and reluctantly got into the car.

'Are you and Katrina back on again?' Nathan asked Alex.

'Yeah. But her mother still hates me. She won't let Katrina see me or talk to me on the phone. It's hopeless. Unless ...'

'Unless what?'

'Could I have the radios back?'

Mrs Muggleton's car stopped outside the city library and Katrina got out with her books. Mrs Muggleton watched her daughter go inside the building, then drove away. As soon as she was gone, Katrina came out. She'd show Paul and Alex. She was going to find Ashka before they did. She checked the front page of the newspaper and hurried away.

The salesman was lifting a television set down from the wall display when Katrina came into the store. 'Sorry. We're closed.'

'I don't want to buy anything.' Katrina took out a pen and opened her notebook. 'I'm doing an article on strange happenings for my high-school newspaper. Could you tell me what happened here?'

'I don't want to be rude but we're very busy. We have to replace all our stock.' He put the set down on a trolley.

'Why is that?'

The salesman turned a switch. The remaining television sets along the wall lit up but every screen was filled with static.

'None of these will ever work again,' the man

said angrily. 'That woman or whatever she was, magnetised every piece of metal in the shop.'

He tossed a handful of paper clips at the TV sets. To Katrina's amazement, they stuck.

Paul and Alex climbed to the top of a hill in a park overlooking the city. They each had a magnetometer and a two-way radio. Paul switched his on and it started beeping.

'We've found her!' Alex crowed.

'That's just the background radiation of the city,' Paul explained, pointing to the radio antennas and satellite dishes that sprouted from the tops of the buildings. 'We have to adjust the meters to ignore their signals. Then if they start beeping, we'll know it's Ashka.'

He carefully turned a dial on the box and the beeping stopped. He did the same with Alex's and handed it back.

'You go that way. I'll go the other. The further apart we are, the better we'll be able to pinpoint Ashka.'

'If she's still here, if she uses the power suit and if these things work,' Alex said.

Paul grinned. 'Yeah.'

Katrina walked down the street, watching the needle on the magnetic compass she had just bought. It pointed north. As she approached the electrical store, the needle swung round and pointed towards the magnetised appliances in the shop.

Katrina continued past the shop and the needle spun round to point at a metal street sign across the road. She excitedly crossed the road and as she passed the sign, the needle swung again and pointed down a lane. Katrina followed the direction of the needle, hot on Ashka's trail.

The magnetic traces led Katrina out of the city to the old oil refinery. It looked creepy and smelled bad but Katrina realised that the maze of metal pipes and storage tanks was an ideal place for Ashka to hide. She squeezed through the narrow gap between the gates and climbed the ladder on the side of a tower. Katrina took her compass out and slowly moved it around. The needle pointed towards a corrugated iron shed below her.

Katrina climbed back down the ladder and warily approached the shed. It looked deserted. Katrina crept around the back. There was something shiny under a rotting tarpaulin. Katrina lifted it and saw a gleaming three-wheeled motorcycle.

Katrina put her ear to the wall of the shed and listened. She heard nothing. She went to the door and turned the handle. It opened with a loud creak.

'Is anyone here?' Katrina called softly as she peered into the gloom.

There was no answer. Katrina moved cautiously into the shed. Behind her, Ashka stepped out of the shadows and energised her power suit. The flash of light made Katrina turn. She stared fearfully at the Spellbinder silhouetted in the doorway, a glowing ball of energy in her hand.

'Alex, are you getting a reading?' Paul said excitedly into his radio. His meter was beeping loudly.

'That's a big roger, Roger,' Alex replied. 'Signal from the northwest with maximum intensity.'

Paul quickly used a ruler to draw lines across his map and carefully checked the coordinates where they intersected. 'I've got it pinpointed at the old refinery,' he told Alex. 'Meet me at reference J24.'

'I copy, dude.'

Paul ran through the park towards the city.

'You *are* a Spellbinder,' Katrina said, half-terrified, half-amazed.

Ashka slammed the shed door shut. 'How do you know about Spellbinders?'

'Paul told me.'

Ashka took a step towards Katrina. 'You know Paul?'

Katrina backed away fearfully. 'Are you Ashka?'

'No ... My name is Marna. I am a Regent of the Spellbinders.' Ashka let the power-bolt fade and smiled at Katrina.

'Paul will be relieved,' Katrina said, starting to relax. 'He thought you were Ashka.'

'Paul knows I'm in this world?'

'Yes. My name's Katrina. Come on, I'll take you to him.' She moved towards the door.

'Wait,' Ashka said. 'How many others has Paul told about my world?'

'No-one. Apart from me and Alex.'

'Good. I need your help, Katrina.'

'To do what?'

'The Regents were both frightened and excited by what Paul told us about his world. I've been sent here to see if it is safe for us to make contact,' Ashka lied. 'Show me what your world is like. In return, perhaps I can show you mine.'

'Will I get to stay in the castle?' Katrina asked eagerly.

Ashka smiled. 'Of course.'

'Radical! I mean yes, I'll help! I'll get you books and videos and introduce you to people.'

Ashka shook her head. 'No-one else must know that I am here.'

'What about Paul?'

'Paul is very young.'

'He's the same age as me.'

'You behave much older.'

Katrina beamed at the compliment.

Ashka took her hands. 'Katrina, my world is small and weak. If your people find out about it, it could be destroyed. You wouldn't want that, would you?'

Katrina shook her head. 'It'll be our secret. The first thing is to get you somewhere decent to stay.'

Paul and Alex dismally surveyed the abandoned refinery. Their magnetometers were useless unless Ashka used her power suit again; she could be hidden anywhere in the maze of pipes and tanks. Alex pointed at the old shed. 'Maybe she's in there.'

The boys warily approached and Paul carefully opened the door. There was no-one inside. Alex noticed the ashes in the hubcap on the floor and held his hand over them. 'These are warm. Someone's been here.'

Paul saw the empty stew can with the spoon sticking out of it. He picked up the can and the spoon slid out. It stopped, hanging magnetically from the lip of the can.

'Ashka was here,' Paul said.

Katrina sat behind Ashka on the motorbike, laughing with exhilaration. She'd never been on one before. 'I can't believe you taught yourself to ride this.'

'It's a lot simpler than one of our flying ships,' Ashka said, dropping down a gear and roaring up the hill.

Katrina pointed to the hotel where her parents stayed when they wanted a weekend to themselves, and Ashka pulled into the kerb. They got off the bike and removed their helmets.

'What are we going to do about money?' Katrina asked.

Ashka took out the bank notes she had stolen from the electrical shop. 'Will this do?'

Katrina stared at the thick wad and smiled. 'I don't think you need my help at all.'

'I do. Without you I'm lost.' Ashka handed Katrina the money.

'Let me handle everything,' Katrina said. 'Just remember you're my aunt from Iceland and you don't speak English.'

She took Ashka's hand and led her into the hotel.

A short time later, Katrina opened the door of the hotel room and ushered Ashka in. The Spellbinder stared in amazement at the view over the city from the high window. 'We have nothing like this in my world.'

'You'll get used to it. This is called a TV. You operate it with this.' Katrina picked up the remote control and turned the TV on and off. 'And this is the telephone. If you want anything to eat, just pick it up, push this button and ask for room service. This explains how everything in the hotel works.' She opened the hotel directory.

Ashka looked at the strange words. 'I can't read your writing.'

Katrina frowned. 'That's going to make it hard to learn about this world.' Then she noticed the VCR beneath the TV. 'You've got a video recorder! I'll borrow a whole lot of tapes from the school library and bring them tomorrow. I'll get you stuff on history and art and music and ...'

'Not just the good things,' Ashka interrupted. 'I need to know about the bad things as well.'

Katrina noticed the clock beside the bed. 'I have to go now. Will you be alright?'

'Yes. Thank you, Katrina. I look forward to showing you my world.'

Ashka ushered Katrina out of the door and

closed it. The smile disappeared from her face and she picked up the phone.

'Yes,' the receptionist answered.

'Bring me food!'

Katrina was waiting outside the library when her mother's car pulled up. Katrina ran over and got in. 'Great hair, Mum,' she enthused. 'It really suits you.'

'Thank you. Did you get much study done?'

'Heaps. It's so quiet and there're so many books, you feel like you're absorbing knowledge through your skin. I wish I could study here every night after school.'

'I think that can be arranged.'

Mrs Muggleton started the car. Katrina smiled to herself.

Alex sat on a bench in the schoolyard, desperately trying to finish his homework before the bell rang. 'What's the answer to question 7?' he asked Paul.

Paul was staring into space. 'Why do you think Ashka's here?'

'Paul,' Alex said impatiently, 'how am I ever

going to improve my grades if you don't tell me the answers?'

Paul saw Katrina come into the yard and hurried over to her. Alex groaned and went after him.

'We found out where Ashka is,' Paul said excitedly.

Katrina stared at him in surprise, wondering how he had found out about the hotel.

'We think she's hiding at an old refinery,' Alex said.

Katrina smiled with relief.

'We're going to stake it out after school,' Paul told her. 'Do you want to come?'

'I can't.'

'But I thought you wanted to see a Spellbinder.'

'I'm too busy.'

'Doing what?' Alex asked.

'Getting an education. You should try it.' Katrina turned away and marched towards the school library.

'What's wrong with her?' Alex asked.

After school, Katrina's mother drove her to the

city library to study. Once she was gone, Katrina hurried to Ashka's hotel. Hidden under the books in her bag were a selection of her mother's dresses.

Ashka took a floral print dress into the bathroom to get changed.

'If you don't like any of these, I can bring some more,' Katrina said, laying the other dresses out on the bed. 'Mum's got so many dresses, she'll never miss one or two.'

Ashka came out of the bathroom wearing the dress. She looked very uncomfortable. 'Why does your mother have so many clothes?'

'She likes to look fashionable.'

'Fashionable?'

'Yeah, clothing styles keep changing,' Katrina explained. 'You have to look up-to-date. Men like it.'

Ashka looked at herself in the mirror. 'Do I look fashionable?'

'You could, Marna. If you'd relax a bit.'

'It's this dress. It makes me feel so ... vulnerable. Perhaps if I put this on.' Ashka went to get the power suit hanging in the wardrobe.

'No,' Katrina said, 'you'll get used to it. Walk up and down a bit. Imagine you're gliding.'

Ashka walked around the room, trying to glide. She looked stiff and awkward. Katrina struggled not to laugh. 'Keep practising.'

Katrina went over to the TV and started going through the stack of videotapes she had borrowed from her school library. 'What tape do you want to watch?'

'You choose one.' Ashka picked up a book of news photographs and turned the pages. She stopped at a photo of a sinister-looking aircraft. 'What's this?'

'It's a stealth bomber.'

'What does it do?'

Katrina sighed. How was she going to explain the war-like tendencies of her world without scaring the Spellbinder?

In the refinery, Paul and Alex kept watch on the shed from behind a stack of pallets.

'Face it, mate,' Alex said impatiently. 'Ashka's not coming back here.'

'You don't know that.'

'You don't even know that it was Ashka.'

This is a total waste of time.' Alex got up.

'If you stay,' Paul said quickly, 'I'll help you with your homework for a whole week.'

'Two.'

'OK,' Paul agreed grudgingly.

Alex grinned and sat down again. 'Make sure you finish your maths assignment tonight. I'll get it off you at lunchtime.'

'You can't.' Paul pointed to their magnetometers. 'We're measuring the electro-magnetic radiation around the school, remember.'

Alex groaned.

'What do you want me to bring tomorrow?' Katrina asked Ashka as they came out of the hotel.

'Can you bring a tape that will tell me more about your weapons?'

'Why are you so interested in weapons? There's much more interesting stuff than that.'

Before Ashka could answer, a large grey van pulled up on the street in front of them. Its riveted-metal body and thick glass windows reminded Ashka of a Spellbinder flying ship.

'What is that?'

'A security van. They're delivering money to the hotel.'

'Will they deliver some to me?'

Katrina laughed. 'You could try asking but I don't fancy your luck. See you tomorrow.' Katrina walked away.

A man in uniform got out of the cab and went to the back of the van. He unlocked a door and another man got out, carrying a heavy leather satchel. Ashka watched curiously as the men went into the hotel.

'Look out, here come the ghostbusters,' Giannos cackled, as Paul and Alex crossed the schoolyard, scanning the buildings with their magnetometers. The lunchtime crowd of students laughed as Giannos and Smithy capered around Paul and Alex, wailing like ghosts.

'Get lost, Smithy,' an embarrassed Alex growled, 'or you will be a ghost.'

Smithy and Giannos kept up their taunting until Ms Gibson appeared. 'How's it going, boys?' she asked.

'We're not picking up much radiation,' Paul told her.

Ms Gibson smiled. 'Well that's a relief. It means our brains are safe. Alex, I'm very pleased to see you involved in this. I'd like you both to write up your methods and results in detail and present them to the class.'

As Ms Gibson walked away, Alex glared at Paul. 'I'm going to get you for this, Reynolds.'

Two uniformed guards came out of the rear of a large department store and went to the security van parked in the narrow street behind it. One guard was carrying a heavy leather satchel. He climbed into the back of the van and closed the door behind him. The other guard locked it and then climbed into the front of the van. As he started the engine, Ashka roared into the street on her motorcycle. The guard watched nervously as the black-leather clad figure got off the bike and stood in front of the van. A spark flashed as Ashka struck her wrists together and energised the power suit.

In the schoolyard, both magnetometers started beeping.

'Miss Gibson!' Alex yelled.

'Shut up,' Paul hissed. 'It's Ashka.' He moved the sphere around until the reading on the meter peaked. 'The signal's coming from the city. Come on.'

He and Alex ran towards the gate.

Before the driver of the security van could reach for his radio, Ashka hurled a power-bolt. Energy crackled over the van's metal body, electrifying it. The shock stunned the driver, who slumped forward over the steering wheel.

Ashka went to the rear of the van and fired another bolt. The lock melted and the door sprang open. An unconscious guard tumbled out and lay on the road. Ashka reached into the van and pulled out the leather satchel. She ran back to her bike, leaped on and roared away.

By the time Paul and Alex reached the crime scene, a police car was parked by the security van.

'She fired some kind of laser beam at me,' the dazed driver said to an astonished detective.

'I suppose you're going to tell me it was an alien?' the detective scoffed.

'What else could it be?'

Paul started to go towards the policeman but Alex grabbed him. 'The cop isn't buying the alien story. What makes you think they'll listen if you start blabbing about Spellbinders from another world?'

Paul reluctantly nodded.

'Ashka's broken the law now,' Alex said. 'Let the police find her.'

Back in her hotel room, Ashka began removing the money from the satchel and stacking it in a briefcase. The TV was on loudly and she didn't hear the knock at the door. It opened and a maid came in wheeling a cleaning trolley.

'Excuse me,' the maid said when she saw Ashka.

Startled, Ashka whirled round and energised her power suit.

Paul and Alex were trudging homewards when their magnetometers started beeping. At the same moment, a fire alarm started ringing in the hotel across the street. Paul pointed his meter at the hotel and the needle went into the red zone. He looked excitedly at Alex. 'I think we just found Ashka.'

Clowning Around

Frightened guests and employees streamed out of the hotel in response to the fire alarm. Paul pointed his magnetometer at the building and slowly tilted it up, checking the reading.

'The signal's coming from the top floor,' he told Alex. 'Come on.'

They ran across the road and pushed their way into the lobby. The alarm suddenly stopped and their meters stopped beeping. The hotel staff started ushering the guests back inside.

'Now, how are we going to find out what room she's in?' Alex asked.

At the bottom of the stairs stood a shop dummy dressed in a clown costume. A bunch of helium-filled balloons was tied to one hand. In the other was a sign reading 'Children's Party. Conference Room 1.' Paul looked at the dummy, then at Alex: they were both about the same size.

The lift door opened and Paul stepped out into the empty corridor. He turned back to the lift. 'Alex, come on.'

Alex shuffled out of the lift, wearing the clown suit and holding the bunch of balloons. His cheeks were red with embarrassment, almost as red as the nose he was wearing. 'Why do *I* have to wear this?' he grumbled.

'Because Ashka knows *me*. Go on.' Paul pushed Alex towards the nearest door and knocked, ducking back out of sight as a woman opened it.

'Hi there, I'm lucky Lexo,' Alex said lamely.

'How can I help you?' the woman asked in surprise.

Alex glanced at Paul, who shook his head. 'You can't. Sorry, wrong room.'

The woman shut the door.

'Try the next one,' Paul said. 'And this time, smile.'

Ashka transferred the last of the stolen

money from the satchel to the briefcase and shut it. There was a knock at the door. She quickly slid the bags under the bed and went to answer it.

'Hidey hidey ho!' Alex chortled as Ashka opened the door. 'I'm Lucky Lexo, the hotel clown.'

Ashka shut the door in his face.

'That was her,' Paul hissed from behind a potted plant. 'Try again.'

Alex banged on the door. Ashka wrenched it open. Alex smiled and held up the key to his house. 'If your room key matches this special prize key,' Alex said before Ashka could protest, 'you win one week's free accommodation. Isn't that great?'

Ashka tried to shut the door again but Alex stopped it with his foot. 'If I don't check all the keys, I'll lose my job,' he said pathetically. 'My mum's sick and my dad ran off. I've got six sisters and ...'

'Alright!' Ashka gave him her room key. Alex held it up against his key and pretended to compare them.

'Sorry, wrong key. But you still get the

consolation prize.' He held out the bunch of balloons. As Ashka reached for them, Alex let them go. Ashka was fascinated by the brightly coloured balloons and watched as they floated up to the ceiling. While she was distracted, Alex quickly switched the room key for his own.

'Here's your key. Bye.' Alex handed it back and hurried away.

A few minutes later, Paul came out of the lift and crossed the lobby to the row of house phones. Still wearing the clown suit, Alex peeked out of the lift at the hotel doorman who was scratching his head in bewilderment as he stared at the naked dummy. Alex dived out of the lift and took cover behind a palm tree. Paul picked up the phone and dialled.

'Yes,' Ashka answered.

'Ashka, this is Paul.'

'How did you find me?' Ashka asked in surprise.

'This is my world, remember. Meet me across the road from the hotel.' He hung up and went over to Alex. 'She's on her way.'

Inside the hotel, Ashka came out of her room and went to the lift. As the door closed behind her, Paul and Alex emerged from the stairwell and hurried to her room. Alex took Ashka's key from the pocket of his clown suit and unlocked the door.

'Keep watch,' Paul said as he followed Alex inside. 'I'll check the room.'

Alex closed the door to a crack and peered through it. Paul opened the wardrobe and grinned. 'I've got the power suit.'

'Then let's get out of here,' Alex begged.

'No. We've got to find the money.' Paul started opening the drawers in the dresser.

Alex noticed something protruding from under the bed. He got down on his hands and knees and pulled out the leather satchel and the briefcase. 'Paul,' he hissed.

Paul came over as Alex opened the briefcase. The boys stared in shock at the bundles of bank notes. Alex grabbed a wad. 'Wow! Imagine what we could buy with this!'

'Put it back,' Paul said. 'I'm calling the police.'

As Alex reluctantly replaced the money,

there was a knock at the door. Alex dived behind the bed, leaving Paul standing exposed in the middle of the room. The door swung open and Katrina came in, carrying an armful of picture books and videotapes. She and Paul gaped at each other.

'Katrina!'

'Paul!?'

'Well, that takes care of the introductions,' Alex said, getting up from behind the bed. 'What are you doing here?'

'Me?' Katrina asked. She stared at Alex's colourful costume. 'Why are you dressed like that? What are you doing in Marna's room?'

'Marna?' Paul exclaimed. 'This is Ashka's room.'

'She told me her name was Marna,' Katrina said.

'She was lying.'

'But she's really nice. She's going to take me back to her world ...'

'Katrina, look at this.' Paul opened the briefcase. 'Ashka robbed a security van.'

Katrina stared at the money in shock. She dropped the books and tapes and slumped on

235

the bed. Paul picked up one of the books; the thick volume was entitled *Modern Military Weapons*.

'You're teaching Ashka about weapons, aren't you?' Paul said angrily to Katrina. 'Don't you realise she's here to get knowledge so she can take over Riana's world?'

'I didn't know,' Katrina protested.

'She's coming!' Alex called from the door.

Katrina leaped to her feet. 'Hide in the bathroom. I'll get rid of her.'

Paul quickly pushed the satchel and briefcase back under the bed, then he and Alex hurried into the bathroom and shut the door. Katrina was gathering up the books and tapes when Ashka came in. 'Hi,' she called cheerily.

Ashka closed the door and looked at Katrina suspiciously. 'Did you tell Paul about me?'

'Of course I didn't. Why?'

'How did you get in here?'

'... a maid let me in.'

Ashka opened the wardrobe and was relieved to see the power suit still inside.

'Look at these great books I got,' Katrina

said, holding up the book on weapons. 'Let's go down to the coffee shop and I'll show you.'

'I need to check something first.' Ashka pulled the briefcase from under the bed and went towards the bathroom.

As she turned the handle, the door was wrenched open from the inside. Paul and Alex ran out, throwing a hotel dressing-gown over Ashka's head. As they pushed her across the room, they collided with Katrina, who staggered backwards over the bed and fell off the other side.

Alex struggled to hold Ashka on the bed while Paul took the power suit from the wardrobe. As Paul ran for the door, Alex tried to pull the briefcase from Ashka's hand but she wouldn't let go.

'Leave it,' Paul yelled from the door.

Alex leaped off the bed and raced out after Paul. Ashka threw the dressing-gown off and got up.

'What happened?' Katrina asked innocently from beside the bed. 'Who were they?'

Ashka yanked Katrina to her feet. 'Go home.'

She pushed Katrina into the corridor and recognised Paul running away with the power suit. Ashka realised what had happened. 'You did this!' she roared at Katrina. She saw Paul and Alex racing down the stairs and went after them.

Paul and Alex burst out of the stairwell into the hotel lobby. They slowed and began to walk nonchalantly towards the front door. Alex saw the doorman staring at him and remembered he was still in the clown suit. He pulled Paul back towards the stairs but a lift opened and Ashka stepped out. Paul and Alex were trapped between her and the doorman. Then a party of young children bustled into the hotel.

'Clown! Clown!' they cried when they spotted Alex. In seconds, he and Paul were surrounded by clamouring youngsters.

As Ashka came towards them, Alex noticed a big bowl of chocolates on the reception desk. He grabbed two handfuls. 'Hey, kids, chokkies!' Alex tossed the sweets towards Ashka and the children flocked after them, blocking her way.

Clutching the power suit, Paul ran through a door marked 'STAFF ONLY' and found himself in an alley at the rear of the hotel. A garbage truck blocked the street end. Paul headed the other way but the alley ended in a high brick wall. The door flew open and Ashka ran out. 'Give me the power suit!' she barked.

As Ashka moved towards Paul, Alex came out of the door behind her. He saw the situation and mimed a rugby pass to Paul. Ashka was surprised when Paul started running towards her. When he was a few steps away, Paul threw the suit over Ashka's head to Alex. She whirled round, saw Alex and tackled him. Alex just managed to pass the suit back to Paul as he and Ashka crashed to the ground.

Paul ran to the garbage truck and tossed the power suit in. He hit a green switch on the back of the truck and the garbage compactor started up. Ashka saw the suit being pulled into the grinding jaws of the compactor. She leaped onto the back of the truck and desperately tried to pull it out. Bolts of power crackled around the suit as the powerful compactor began to crush it. Ashka was thrown from the truck and the ruined suit vanished from sight.

Ashka got to her feet and shot a look of hatred at Paul. Behind her, two garbage men came up the side of the truck carrying garbage bags. Ashka quickly pushed past them and ran out into the street. To the garbage men's surprise, Paul started dancing around the alley with Alex, whooping victoriously.

Katrina was outside the hotel looking anxiously up and down the street when Paul and Alex emerged from the alley. 'Where's Ashka?' she asked. 'Did she get the power suit?'

'No way,' Paul crowed. 'We totalled it. There's nothing Ashka can do now.'

'What are we going to do with all that money?' Alex asked eagerly.

'We'll have to give it back,' Paul said.

Alex looked very disappointed.

'There's probably a big fat reward,' Katrina suggested.

Alex grinned. 'Well, what are we waiting for?'

In Ashka's hotel room Paul looked up from under the bed. 'The briefcase is gone.'

'There goes the reward,' Alex moaned.

Katrina checked through the books on the bed. 'The book on weapons is gone too.'

Paul went cold. 'With all that money, Ashka can buy whatever she wants. Why didn't you tell me about her, Katrina?'

'You were too busy fooling around with those stupid detectors. At least I found her.'

'Sure you found her,' Paul said scornfully. 'And she sucked you right in. You think you're so clever. Now Ashka's got away and she could do anything.'

'Paul,' Alex cautioned.

'Stay out of this, Alex.' He turned angrily on Katrina. 'This is all your fault.'

'My fault? You were the one that got us into this mess in the first place. All I've done is try to help.' Katrina choked back a sob and hurried out.

'I think you went too far, buddy,' Alex said.

'It is her fault,' Paul insisted.

'Yeah? If it wasn't for Katrina, you'd still be stuck in the Spellbinders' world. Think about that.' Alex turned his back on Paul and hurried after Katrina.

Alex and Katrina had gone by the time Paul came out of the hotel with the magnetometers. Wondering if he might have been a bit hard on Katrina, Paul began to make his way home. He didn't notice Ashka on her motorcycle across the road. The briefcase was strapped to the seat behind her. As Paul walked away, Ashka started the bike and slowly began to follow him.

Brian and Christine were preparing dinner when Paul clumped into the kitchen.

'Why the long face?' Brian asked, pouring chicken pieces from a bowl into a hot frying pan.

'It's been one of those days.'

'Want to talk?'

Paul shook his head. As the chicken began to sizzle, Christine looked up from a cookbook. 'Dad! You're supposed to brown the onions first.'

Brian quickly tried to tip the chicken pieces

back into the bowl but some fell to the floor.

'How can you be one of the country's top scientists and not be able to read a recipe?' Paul asked as he started to pick them up.

No-one noticed as Ashka's face appeared at the corner of the open kitchen window. She drew back out of sight, listening to the conversation.

'I don't do things the way they're supposed to be done,' Brian said proudly. 'That's why I'm such a success.'

'And such a lousy cook.' Paul dumped the chicken into the bowl. 'Are you working on anything interesting at the moment?'

'Not really. People bring in their designs and I make them more powerful or faster or whatever's required. To tell the truth, I'm a bit bored. I need a new challenge. Which reminds me. I've got to nip back to work and finish off a report. Do you mind helping Christine finish this off?'

Paul shook his head. Dinner would probably taste better if Christine cooked it anyway. Brian picked up his briefcase and went out. Ashka hurried back to her bike.

Brian drove up to the entrance of Magnetronix and beeped his horn. The security guard came out of the hut and waved. As he raised the boom gate, Ashka cruised past on her bike. She watched Brian drive through the entrance, then smiled and accelerated away. Now that she had found Paul's father, she could put her plan into action. But first she had to get back to her own world.

Ashka found her way out of the city but became lost in the countryside around Mount Lara. Tired and frustrated, she stopped at an intersection, wondering which road would lead her back to the cave. She had to get there before nightfall and rehang the cable that Paul had taken down. In the morning, with Gryvon's help, she would open the doorway and return to her world.

Ashka saw an old green car approaching and recognised it as the one that had given Paul a lift. She rode her bike into the middle of the road, blocking the intersection.

The elderly nun stopped her car and rolled down the window as Ashka approached. 'Can I help you?'

'I'm lost,' Ashka said curtly.

The nun shook her head. 'So many people are these days. When I was a novice ...'

'Three days ago,' Ashka cut in, 'I saw a boy get into your car.'

'That would have been at the school camp. I gave him a lift to ...'

'Tell me how to get to this school camp,' Ashka snapped. The elderly nun frowned, not impressed by Ashka's lack of manners. Ashka swallowed her pride and smiled. 'Please. It's an emergency.'

For the third morning in a row, Gryvon trudged up the trail to the Summoning Tower. He was starting to wonder if Ashka would ever return. He placed the Eyestone in position and was surprised when power started to crackle between the tower and the Eyestone. There was a flash as the doorway opened and Ashka stepped through.

'Are you ready to take over the castle?' Gryvon asked eagerly.

245

'Not yet. I need to go back to Paul's world again ... after I've borrowed a few things from the Spellbinders.' She removed the Eyestone from the dish at the base of the tower and the doorway closed.

Gryvon stared at the colourful dress Ashka was wearing. 'Why are you dressed like that?'

'This is how people look in Paul's world. It's a very strange place. You'll have to find me some other clothes.'

'What happened to your power suit?'

Ashka scowled and headed towards the trail leading to Clayhill.

Over breakfast, Christine and Brian discussed the menu for the coming week. Paul was silent, trying to guess what Ashka's next move would be.

'Dad, can we have a barbecue like we used to?' Christine suggested.

'Good idea. How about tomorrow night?'

Paul realised that this could be a good opportunity to patch things up with his friends. 'Can I ask Alex and Katrina?'

'Sure. Would you like to invite someone, Christine?'

'What about Gina?'

'Um ... I don't know. Don't you think she sees enough of us?'

'You can never see too much of someone you like. I'll give her a ring.' Christine hurried out before Brian could argue.

'Are you getting keen on Gina, Dad?' Paul asked.

Brian quickly began to clear the table. 'Don't be silly. It's just a barbecue.'

Paul looked around the schoolyard and found Katrina sitting with Alex. She was helping him with his homework.

'Hi, guys,' Paul said brightly. 'Want to come to a barbecue tomorrow night?'

Katrina got up without looking at Paul. 'Alex, if you want to finish this, I'll be in the library.' She gathered her books and started to leave.

'What's up with her?' Paul asked Alex.

Katrina turned back angrily. 'While you were in Riana's world, I was really worried about you. I guess it was because I liked you. I can't think why.' She stalked away.

'You really hurt her the other day,' Alex said.

'I was angry. I'm sorry.'

'It's not me you should be apologising to. Katrina stuck her neck out for you.' Alex grabbed his books and went after her.

'Katrina! I'm sorry,' Paul yelled. She didn't look back. 'What about the barbecue?'

There was no reply.

Riana walked around the side of the barn, her eye glued to the viewfinder of Paul's video-camera. Through the lens, she saw Gryvon by a washing line strung with clothes. He had something concealed under his cloak.

'Smile, Gryvon,' she called, 'you're on TV.'

Gryvon turned and Riana got a close-up of his guilty face. He pushed past her and hurried out of the village to a clearing in the forest.

There was a tap on his shoulder and Gryvon whirled around. Ashka stood behind him, still wearing Katrina's mother's clothes. Gryvon pulled a red dress from under his tunic. Ashka took it and went behind a tree to get changed. Gryvon took out the Gameboy he had stolen from Riana and started to play with it.

'Keep a lookout,' Ashka snapped. She snatched the electronic toy from Gryvon and tossed it away. The Gameboy hit a tree with a loud crack and fell to the ground, beeping continuously.

'Have you seen Gryvon?' Bron called to Riana from the roof of the nearly completed cottage. 'He's supposed to be helping me.'

'I saw him going into the forest.'

'Probably gone for a nap. I'll give him an earful when he gets back.' Bron resumed hammering.

Maran approached them with an armful of dry washing. 'Did you bring my new dress in?' she asked Riana.

'No, Ma.'

Maran shook her head. 'I washed it yesterday and put it out to dry. Now it's gone.'

Riana remembered Gryvon's guilty look.

A few minutes later, Riana crept carefully through the forest searching for Gryvon. She heard a faint, familiar sound and looked down. The broken Gameboy was lying beneath a tree, still beeping. As Riana picked it up, she noticed something gleaming under a bush. She pushed the branches aside and saw a pair of shiny patent leather shoes. Beside them was a floral print dress. Riana realised they were from Paul's world. She picked up a shoe and hurried back to Clayhill.

'Da, Ma, look!'

Bron and Maran looked up from their work as Riana came running towards them, holding up the shoe.

'What is it?' Bron asked.

'A shoe.'

'Doesn't look very comfortable,' Maran remarked. 'Where did you get it?'

'I found it in the forest. I think Ashka's been to Paul's world. Gryvon must have stolen your dress so Ashka could change clothes.'

'Where is Gryvon now?' Bron asked.

'He must have gone with Ashka. I have to tell Correon.'

Bron and Maran exchanged glances, uneasy at the prospect of Riana becoming involved with the Spellbinders again.

'Tell the Summoner,' Bron suggested. 'He'll send a message to the castle.'

'Do *you* want to tell him that his son's helping Ashka again?' Riana asked. Bron shook his head. 'Then I have to go to the castle.'

'No, Riana,' Bron said. 'It's not your problem.'

'But Ashka's been to Paul's world,' Riana argued. 'She might have brought back something dangerous.'

'Let her go, Bron,' Maran said. 'She's doing what she thinks is right. You taught her that.'

Hidden in the undergrowth overlooking the Spellbinders' castle, Gryvon smeared mud and leaves over his clothes and face. 'What if Correon doesn't believe me?' he asked Ashka.

'You'll just have to make sure he does.' She ripped open the front of his tunic. 'Now it looks like you've been on the run. Get as many powerstones as you can. I'll meet you at the ruins.' She disappeared into the trees.

Gryvon stepped onto the track and began

251

staggering towards the castle gate. 'Help,' he cried.

A sentry came out of the guard hut. Gryvon collapsed to his knees. 'I must speak to Regent Correon,' he moaned. 'I've seen Ashka.'

Gryvon limped along the corridor, supported by a burly guard. 'I'll be alright now,' he said as they reached the door to Correon's apartment. The guard left. Gryvon threw the door open and staggered in.

'Regent Corr ...' Gryvon stared in surprise at Zander, who was sitting at Correon's desk. Zander stared back at him, equally surprised.

'You're a Marauder!' Gryvon cried.

'You destroyed our camp!' Zander scrambled from behind the desk and leaped on Gryvon. They crashed to the floor and wrestled, knocking over piles of books.

'Stop that,' Correon roared from the door. 'I'm trying to bring peace between the Marauders and the Spellbinders and you're fighting in my room.'

Gryvon and Zander got to their feet, still glaring at each other. Correon noticed the mud on Gryvon's torn clothes.

'What happened to you? What are you doing here?'

'Ashka attacked me near Clayhill. She hit me with a power-bolt but I escaped and ran here. She's gone mad. She said she's going to wipe out the Marauders.'

'You promised us it was safe to come out of the mountains,' Zander angrily reminded Correon.

'We must warn Kurn and the others,' the Spellbinder said. 'Where's Ashka now?'

'I don't know.'

'We'll take a flying ship. Gryvon, get some rest. You've done well.'

'Thank you, Regent.' Gryvon went to a couch and lay down. As soon as Correon and Zander left, he got up and looked around the room. There were jars of liquids and powders on a shelf. Gryvon quickly began sorting through them.

Gryvon crept along the tunnel and into the power chamber beneath the castle. He crouched by the entrance to the cage that surrounded the massive powerstone arch. Two Apprentices wheeled a trolley of powerstones beneath the arch. They moved back to a safe distance as energy began to crackle from the arch to the trolley, recharging the depleted stones.

Gryvon opened his bag and took out two jars. He poured sulphur from one and iron filings from the other into a pile on the floor. Gryvon mixed them together as he had seen Paul do when he made the gas that smelt like rotten eggs. He covered his nose and mouth with a damp cloth, then took a flaming torch from the wall and held the flame over the pile of chemicals. It started to smoulder, giving off thick clouds of gas.

The Apprentices fled out of the cage and down the tunnel, gagging and retching from the terrible smell. Holding the cloth over his face, Gryvon hurried over to the arch and began filling his bag with recharged powerstones.

Mort and Borin stood by the guard hut at the castle gate, watching Riana trot towards them. The video-camera was in a bag slung over her shoulder.

'It's that girl again,' Mort moaned.

'That's close enough,' Borin said to Riana. 'What do you want this time?'

'I have to see Regent Correon. It's important.'

Mort pointed to a flying ship disappearing into the distance. 'You just missed him.'

'When will he be back?'

'Mort, my good man,' Borin said sarcastically to his mate, 'the last time you were taking tea with Regent Correon, did he mention when he'd be back from his little jaunt?'

'Sorry. Since I threw up on his best rug, he doesn't tell me a thing.'

The sentries guffawed.

'I'll wait,' Riana said dryly and sat under a tree.

A few moments later, the castle gate opened and Gryvon hurried out. He was carrying a heavy bag and a coil of rope. Riana ducked behind the tree as Gryvon strode past the guard hut and disappeared down the road. Realising she couldn't wait for Correon, she went after Gryvon.

Riana followed him to the old Spellbinder castle. She crept through the ruins, wondering what Gryvon was doing there. Ashka suddenly stepped out from hiding and Riana dropped to the ground.

'Did you get them?' Ashka asked. Gryvon opened his bag and took out a powerstone. 'Good. Show me the vault.'

Gryvon led Ashka through the rubble to the crater produced when Paul had first demonstrated gunpowder to Ashka. Gryvon tied his rope around a heavy rock and dropped the end down the hole at the bottom of the crater. Carefully he climbed down the rope into the vault beneath the ruins.

Gryvon lit a torch and held it up while Ashka climbed down the rope. She stared at the white bones lying around the gloomy vault. 'So these are the old Spellbinders,' Ashka said contemptuously. 'They don't look so powerful now. Where's the book?'

Gryvon jammed the torch into a crack in the wall above a desk covered in dusty books. He hunted through them and picked up a thick octagonal volume. 'Look,' he said, opening it and pointing to a page. 'It shows how to build power suits and flying ships.'

As Ashka and Gryvon pored over the diagrams in the old book, Riana quietly slid down the rope to the floor of the vault. She took cover behind a skeleton sitting on a chair. Riana carefully lifted the video-camera from her bag and started to film.

Ashka closed the book. 'I'll take this to Paul's world,' she said excitedly. 'Their scientists will be able to improve these designs with their computers. When I come back, no-one will be able to stand against me. I'll rule the Spellbinders.'

Riana shifted her weight and leaned against the skeleton. It collapsed, the bones clattering loudly on the floor. Ashka and Gryvon whirled round. Riana leaped to her feet and ran for the rope but Ashka caught her.

'She heard everything,' Gryvon said.

'Then she'll have to stay here, won't she? Hold her.'

Gryvon grabbed Riana, and Ashka climbed back up the rope.

'Gryvon, think what you're doing,' Riana pleaded.

257

'I know what I'm doing. I want to be a Spellbinder.'

'If the Regents find out what you're up to, they'll banish you,' Riana warned him.

'They're not going to find out, are they?'

Gryvon pushed Riana across the vault. He quickly climbed up the rope and out of the hole. Riana lunged for the rope but Gryvon pulled it out of reach and disappeared from sight. Riana stared up at the hole, wondering how she was going to get out.

Ashka and Gryvon reappeared, carrying a large rock. 'You should have stayed in Clayhill, Riana,' Ashka said. They dropped the rock over the hole, sealing it.

By the light of the flickering torch, Riana desperately dragged a desk to the centre of the vault and balanced a chair on it. She started to climb but the rotted desk collapsed and Riana crashed to the floor in a cloud of dust. The torch went out and the vault was plunged into darkness.

The High-Tech Power Suit

Paul feinted and dodged around Brian. He dribbled the basketball along the path, jumped and shot. The ball bounced off the backboard and just missed Christine, who was coming out of the house carrying a stack of plates.

'Paul, you said you'd get the barbecue ready,' Christine said angrily. 'Gina will be here any minute. Dad, you said you were going to put on your new shirt.' She put the plates on the patio table and went back inside.

'Don't you think Gina's a bit young for you, Dad?' Paul asked.

'She likes me. I don't know any other women who like me. And Christine's getting to that age when she needs a woman's influence in her life.'

'But what have you got in common?'

Before Brian could answer, Christine came

out of the house with Gina. She had dressed for the occasion and looked very attractive in long skirt and high heels.

'Come in, Gina,' Brian said. 'I mean out.' He laughed nervously.

Christine led Gina over to Brian. 'Doesn't Gina look pretty, Dad?' she asked.

'Er ... Yes ... gorgeous. Very nice.'

'Dad bought a new shirt,' Christine said, looking meaningfully at Brian.

'I'll go and put it on. Make yourself at home.' Brian hurried inside.

'I used to have a necklace like that,' Christine said, pointing to the thin silver chain around Gina's neck. 'I gave it to a girl called Riana.'

'That's an unusual name,' Gina said. 'Where's she from?'

'A parallel world.'

Gina stared at Christine.

'Don't mind her,' Paul said quickly, 'she's always making stuff up.' He pulled Christine away.

'You mustn't talk about Riana. Ever.'

'Why?'

'Because it's a secret. We have to forget about Riana. We'll never see her again.'

In the darkness of the vault, a spark flared as Riana struck her flint against steel. The ember landed on a pile of pages torn from a book. Riana blew on it and the tiny flame grew. Riana fed the fire with pieces of broken furniture. She picked up a burning chair leg and looked around the vault. There was no other way out.

A long pole sticking out of a pile of rubble gave her an idea. She pulled it free and tried to push away the rock that sealed the hole above her head. The rock was too heavy and the pole slipped off, digging into the surrounding dirt. A shower of earth fell on Riana's head and a thin ray of sunlight appeared. Riana frantically began jabbing the pole into the earth around the rock. Suddenly, an avalanche of dirt fell and Riana leaped backwards. The rock crashed down onto the floor of the vault and sunlight streamed in through the hole.

Riana jammed the pole into a crack in the
stone floor of the vault, then rested the top
end against the edge of the hole. She slung the
video-camera bag over her shoulder and began
to shin up the pole.

The sun was setting by the time Riana returned
to the Spellbinder castle. A horse was tethered
outside the guard hut where the sentries Borin
and Mort were on duty.

'Don't tell me,' Borin sighed as Riana
approached, 'you want to see Regent Correon
because you've got something important to
tell him?' Riana nodded. 'Let me guess. The
sky is about to fall?'

'I know where Ashka is,' Riana said urgently.
'The Spellbinders are in danger.'

'Really? All the Spellbinders are in danger
from one woman?'

'Correon's not here,' Mort said to Riana. 'Go
back to your village.'

Riana knew she'd never be able to catch up
with Ashka on foot. 'I need a flying ship,' she
said.

Borin and Mort went into hysterics at the

ludicrous idea. They staggered back into the guard hut, laughing. Riana stared at the horse: if she couldn't have a flying ship, she'd take the next best thing.

Riana clambered awkwardly into the saddle. She'd never been on a horse before. 'Come on,' she hissed. 'Go!' The horse didn't move.

An Apprentice came out of the guard hut and saw Riana. 'Stop her,' he shouted.

As Mort and Borin ran out of the hut, Riana dug her heels into the horse's flanks. It whinnied and reared. Riana clung desperately to its neck as the horse raced away from the castle.

'Gina would like another glass of wine, Dad,' Christine called. Brian left Paul looking after the steaks on the barbecue and took a bottle to Gina.

'So ... er, what do you like to do?' he asked, filling her glass.

'I used to be into parachuting but then I discovered hang-gliding. Have you ever tried it?'

'No. It's a bit physical for me.'

'It's a rush. You'd love it. Why don't you come with me on the weekend?'

'I don't think I can,' Brian said, trying to sound disappointed. 'We're doing some very exciting work with low-temperature electronics. Do you know that the theoretical efficiency of a low-temperature circuit is close to 100 per cent?'

'Is that right?' Gina said, trying to sound interested.

There was an awkward silence.

'Try one of these,' Christine said, holding out a covered plate. Brian gratefully took it and Christine removed the cover. The sandwiches and savouries were all cut into heart shapes. Brian's cheeks went red with embarrassment.

'Why don't you put some music on?' Paul said, pushing Christine towards the stereo.

Gina smiled at Brian. 'Now's my chance to find out whether you can really dance or not.'

'On a scale of one to ten, I'm a minus five,' Brian warned her.

Music suddenly blared from the speakers,

startling Brian, who spilled savouries and wine over his new shirt and Gina's skirt. 'Christine,' he yelled, 'that was stupid!'

Christine burst into tears and fled across the garden. Brian started to go after her but Gina stopped him. 'Let me talk to her.' She went after Christine.

'You were right,' Brian said to Paul. 'This isn't going to work. How can I tell Gina without hurting her feelings?'

'How should I know? You're the grown-up. Tell her the truth.'

Brian sighed and went over to where Gina and Christine were talking.

'Um ... Gina,' Brian began, 'I ... uh ...'

'Dad,' Christine said awkwardly. 'I hope this won't hurt your feelings but ... Gina reckons you're too old for her.'

Paul burst out laughing. Brian and Gina looked at each other, then did the same. Christine scowled.

Morning mist swirled over the surface of the

stream as Arla filled her bucket with water. She was heading back towards her cottage when she heard the sound of hooves on the wooden bridge. Arla couldn't believe her eyes when her sister Riana reined in a horse beside her. The horse and Riana were streaked with dust and sweat from the long ride.

'What are you doing on a horse?' Arla shrieked.

'I haven't got time to explain. Ashka's trying to get to Paul's world. Get Da and meet me at the Summoning Tower. Run!'

Arla dropped her bucket and ran towards the cottage. Ignoring the astonished looks of the villagers, Riana spurred the horse away from Clayhill.

Ashka placed her Eyestone in position at the base of the Summoning Tower. Power crackled between the tower and the Eyestone and, with a flash, the doorway to Paul's world opened.

'Remember,' Ashka said to Gryvon. 'You must do this every day at dawn.'

Gryvon nodded and handed Ashka the bag containing the old Spellbinder book and the powerstones he had stolen from the castle. Ashka stepped through the doorway and disappeared.

As Gryvon was about to retrieve the Eyestone, a horse galloped out of the rocks, heading straight for the doorway. Gryvon ran to turn it away before it could go through. While Gryvon's back was turned, Riana raced out of the rocks and dived through the doorway.

Riana rolled to her feet and looked quickly around. Ashka was at the edge of the clearing, lifting her briefcase from its hiding place among the rocks. As Ashka turned, Riana ducked into the cave.

The energy doorway disappeared. Ashka pulled down the cable from the cave mouth and hid it under some leaves at the base of the tree. Carrying the briefcase, she headed down the trail towards the school camp. Riana followed her.

As Riana reached the bottom of the trail, she

heard the sound of a powerful motor. She ran into the camp, just in time to see Ashka roaring away on her motorcycle.

Ashka rode along the busy suburban road, going over her plan. With the help of Paul's father, she would build a new power suit and return, invincible, to the Spellbinders' land. Suddenly, the motorcycle began to jerk. The engine spluttered and stopped. Ashka pushed the starter button but the bike refused to go. She steered it to the side of the road, stopping outside a used car yard. A salesman was polishing a gleaming red sports car in the driveway. 'Having some trouble?' he called.

'The Harley won't go,' Ashka said angrily, pushing the starter button again.

'Did you put any petrol in it?' the salesman asked.

Ashka looked blankly at him. 'Petrol?'

'You know: gas ... go juice.'

'Where can I get some? I've got money.'

Ashka unstrapped the briefcase from the seat and opened it. The salesman gaped at the piles of bank notes. He quickly recovered his composure and smiled. 'An attractive woman like you shouldn't be riding around on a bike,' he said persuasively. 'That's more your style.' He pointed to the sports car.

'Are they difficult to drive?' Ashka asked, admiring the sleek vehicle.

'Absolutely not,' the salesman promised, taking her arm. 'I could teach you in no time at all. For cash, I'll even throw in a mobile phone.'

Riana hurried into the small country town. She had to find Paul and warn him about Ashka. To her relief, there was a train waiting at the railway station. She hurried to the ticket office. 'I have to catch the train to the city,' she told the ticket seller.

'That'll be four dollars,' he replied.

'I don't have any money. But I have to get to the city.'

'No money, no ticket,' the man snapped. 'Next.'

'I'll pay,' a voice said.

Riana turned and stared at the middle-aged man behind her. He bought two tickets. 'Next

269

time you see someone without any money, you can pay for them.' Riana smiled gratefully as he handed her a ticket.

The research laboratory at Magnetronix was almost completely filled by a huge steel-mesh cage. Brian was inside it, assembling some test equipment, when the phone rang. He stalked out of the cage and picked it up. 'Reynolds ... I can't see anyone right now ... Tell them to make an appointment ... alright. I'm coming. But it had better be important.' He slammed the phone down and stalked out.

'I can't give you long,' Brian said irritably as he pushed open his office door. Ashka was standing by his desk with her back to him. Her flaming red hair was elegantly styled and she wore a figure-hugging black dress. She turned and Brian couldn't help staring. She was beautiful.

'My name is Harley,' Ashka said. 'My husband was ... a person who dug in the ground for old things. I am from Iceland. I don't know your word for this.'

'Archaeologist,' Brian offered.

'Yes. Archaeologist. On our last trip, under an old castle, we found this.' She picked up the old Spellbinder book from the desk. 'My husband was very excited by our find but soon after we found the book, he came down with a fever and died.'

'I'm sorry to hear that,' Brian said. 'But why bring it to me?'

'My husband believed the book contained ancient and powerful secrets. He said we would need a clever scientist to decipher them.'

Brian smiled at the compliment and Ashka held out the book. Brian opened the strange octagonal volume and looked at the unfamiliar writing. 'What language is this?'

'From Iceland. But very old. I can read it but I don't understand the science.'

Brian stared at a page. 'This looks like the wiring diagram for a voltage amplifier. How old is the book?'

'At least 200 years.'

'That's ridiculous. This kind of circuitry wasn't possible then.'

'We also found this.'

Ashka opened her bag and took out a

gleaming rectangular stone. 'The book calls this a powerstone. It is the energy source for this, which is called a power suit.' She pointed to the diagram which showed a similar stone attached to the suit.

Intrigued, Brian took a multimeter from his desk and touched the stone with the probes. Smoke started to rise from the meter and the probes glowed red with heat. Brian quickly lifted them away.

'That packs a heck of a charge,' he exclaimed. 'I've never heard of a battery that small and powerful.'

'If we work together, I'm sure we can unlock its secret.' Ashka moved closer to Brian. 'Will you help me?' she asked softly.

Brian nervously cleared his throat. 'I'd be delighted.'

Ashka smiled. 'The knowledge in this book could be very valuable,' she warned him. 'You must promise to keep it to yourself.'

'Don't worry, Mrs Harley,' Brian promised. 'I won't tell a soul.'

'Why won't you talk to me?' Paul asked as he

followed Katrina into the classroom. Katrina ignored him and went to her seat.

'You shouldn't have blamed her for what happened with Ashka,' Alex reminded him.

Mr Kennett came in and Paul and Alex took their seats. The teacher lifted a pile of test papers from his briefcase. 'The moment you've all been waiting for,' he announced. 'Your maths results.'

The class groaned. Mr Kennett picked a paper from the top of the pile. 'Alex Katsonis. Stand up.'

Alex sighed and stood.

'There are 16 men standing in a row,' Mr Kennett said, '4 of them have dogs. Of the total number of legs on the ground, what fraction are the dogs' legs?'

'But sir, the test question said 12 men and 3 dogs,' Alex protested.

'If you can't work it out,' the teacher said maliciously, 'I'll have to assume you cheated.'

Alex concentrated. 'A half,' he finally answered. 'No, a third, sir.'

'That's correct,' Mr Kennett said with surprise. 'Have you had a brain transplant?'

'No, sir. I asked, but my dad said he couldn't afford it this year.'

The class laughed. Mr Kennett held up Alex's test paper. 'Congratulations: you got a B.'

Alex punched the air. 'Yes!'

As Alex went to collect his paper, Katrina held up her hand and Alex gave her a high five. Paul watched jealously.

'I can't help it if Dad's too old,' Paul snapped at Christine. The argument had started the moment he had got home from school.

'But Gina would have made a great mum!' Christine protested, still upset at the outcome of last night's barbecue.

'Well, we're all in a good mood, aren't we?' Brian said as he came in the front door. Paul and Christine said nothing.

'I don't want to see any long faces tonight,' Brian told them. 'We're going out to dinner. I want to celebrate.'

'Why?' Christine asked.

'I've got a new project to work on. It's fantastic. It might even make us rich.'

Christine cheered.

'What is it?' Paul asked.

'I can't say just at the moment. Mrs Harley wants it kept a secret.'

'Who's Mrs Harley?' Christine asked.

'The woman who brought me the project. Her husband died and she wants me to help finish their work.'

'Is she pretty?'

Brian sighed. 'Yes, but every woman I meet is not a potential marriage partner. Mrs Harley is just a client. Stop trying to run my life. Now, are you coming or not?'

It was dark by the time Riana jogged into Paul's street. She ran to Paul's front door and knocked. There was no answer. Disappointed, she went to the rear of the house. The back door was locked. Riana looked up. Paul's bedroom window was open.

'That seafood pizza was yucky,' Christine complained as she got out of the car. 'Can we have pepperoni next time? ... Dad?'

Brian was lost in his thoughts as he

unlocked the front door and went into the house.

'Dad, look,' Paul said loudly, 'there's a dinosaur on the sofa.'

Brian blinked and stared at him. Paul chuckled. 'Dad, you've been off with the pixies all the way home. What's wrong?'

'Do you two mind if I go back to the lab for a couple of hours?' Brian asked. 'I want to check on something.'

Paul sighed. 'Sure, Dad. See you in the morning.'

Brian smiled guiltily. 'Thanks. Bye.' He went out.

'Do you reckon we'll ever have a normal life?' Christine asked.

Paul shrugged. 'What's normal? Now go and clean your teeth.'

'Make me,' Christine said playfully.

Paul eventually got Christine to bed, and went into his bedroom yawning. He opened the wardrobe to get his pyjamas and let out a yelp of surprise. Riana was inside, asleep. Paul shook her. 'Riana?' She opened her eyes. 'What are you doing here?'

'Ashka's in your world,' Riana said grimly.

'I know that. Alex, Katrina and I destroyed her power suit two days ago.'

'But she's got the old Spellbinder book. She's going to use the science of your world to build a stronger power suit. Then she will go back and defeat the Spellbinders. You have to help me stop her.'

Paul collapsed onto his bed and groaned.

Brian was hunched over a bench in his laboratory, deftly soldering a microprocessor onto a circuit board. The old Spellbinder book was open beside him. He was checking the circuit diagram when a woman in a white lab coat came in. She was carrying a harness of black webbing covered with heavy wiring and electronic circuitry.

'Good work, Anna,' Brian said. 'Put it on the stand.'

Anna draped the prototype power suit over a dressmaker's dummy. Brian finished the circuit board and inserted it into a housing on the belt of the harness. He slotted the powerstone into place behind it and snapped the cover shut.

Everything was ready. Brian threw a switch on the belt and a red light went on.

'Very pretty,' Anna said dryly. 'Can it tap-dance too?'

Suddenly, all the electronic equipment in the laboratory went berserk. Computer screens flashed on and off, light bulbs exploded and an alarm began to wail. Brian quickly turned the switch off and the laboratory returned to normal. He and Anna stared at the harness in shock.

'What is it?' Anna whispered.

Paul hurried into Christine's bedroom and threw the blinds open. Sunlight streamed in through the window and Christine buried her head under her pillow.

'Christine, wake up,' Paul called. 'You've got to go to school.'

Christine groaned. 'I don't feel so good. I think it was that pizza. Can I stay home?'

'Dad's not here and I'm going to school. You can't stay home on your own.'

Christine pulled the covers over her head. Paul threw them off the bed. 'You'll get over it once you're up. Get dressed.'

Paul stood by the front door and waved as Christine trudged grumpily away. As soon as she was out of sight, Paul whistled and Riana came downstairs.

'How are we going to find Ashka?' she asked.

'We'll start at the hotel where she was staying,' Paul said. 'Maybe she went back there.'

Brian ushered Ashka into the laboratory. Anna stepped away from the dressmaker's dummy and Ashka got her first look at the new power suit. Brian and Anna had worked through the night to transfer the components from the harness to a sleek, black leather tunic. Modern technology had turned the old Spellbinder design into a computerised high-tech power suit.

'Thanks for everything, Anna,' Brian said to his assistant. 'Go home and get some sleep.' Anna nodded her thanks and left.

'You must have worked all night, Mr Reynolds,' Ashka said.

279

'It's Brian Reynolds. You can call me Brian.'

'Of course,' Ashka said, 'you have two names.'

Brian looked puzzled.

'You can call me ... Anna. Yes, I have the same name as your servant.'

Brian chuckled. 'Don't call her that when she's around.'

'I'd like to try the suit on,' Ashka said. 'Would you help me?'

Brian took the suit off the dummy and helped Ashka into it. It fitted perfectly.

'How do you make it work?' Ashka asked, looking for the energising plates on the wrists of the suit.

Brian pointed to the switch on the belt. Ashka reached for it but Brian grabbed her hand. 'No! We powered it up last night and nearly blew every circuit in the lab. Try it in there.' He pointed to the huge metal cage. Ashka eyed it warily.

'Don't worry,' Brian reassured her. 'That's a Faraday cage. It confines electro-magnetic radiation. Any energy the suit generates will stay inside it.'

Ashka realised that the cage served the same purpose as the one in the power chamber in the Spellbinder castle. She stepped through the door and Brian closed it. A cable ran from a magnetic field sensor in the cage to a computer. Brian checked the readings on the screen. 'OK, turn it on.'

Ashka turned the switch on the belt. Brian looked at the readings on his screen and his eyebrows went up in surprise. 'The suit produces an incredibly powerful magnetic field. That's enough for now. Come out.'

Ashka ignored him. A glowing ball of energy appeared in her hand. She hurled it at the sensor, which melted in a shower of sparks. Brian stared, gaping in shock. Ashka switched off the power suit and smiled at him. 'I don't know how to thank you for what you have done.'

Uncertain of exactly what he had done, Brian went into the cage and replaced the sensor. Leaving his tools behind, he came out and went back to the computer. 'Turn it on again.'

Ashka threw the switch and energised the

power suit. A heavy spanner flew into her hand, attracted by the suit's powerful magnetic field.

'I didn't think it would do that,' Ashka said in surprise.

'Neither did I.' Brian hurried back into the cage with a large magnet. 'Try it again with this.'

Ashka energised the suit and pointed at the magnet. It flew out of Brian's hand, ripped through the mesh of the cage and slammed into the laboratory wall.

'Yes!' Brian yelled.

Ashka turned off the suit. 'Why did it do that?'

'Because the suit and the magnet repelled each other.' Brian's eyes lit up.

'What is it?' Ashka asked.

'If we built a suit that could generate enough power,' Brian said excitedly, 'it would repel the earth's magnetic field. Then the suit would be able to fly!'

Ashka was astounded. This was more than she had hoped for. Before she could ask more, the phone rang. Brian picked it up.

'Brian Reynolds ... What? Is she alright? ... No, I'll come and get her right away.' He put down the phone, looking worried. 'My daughter is sick. I have to pick her up from school and take her home. I don't think I'll be able to come back today.'

Ashka hid her frustration. 'Poor girl. Do you have any other children?'

'Yes, I've a son, Paul. Listen, why don't you meet me at my house later? Then I can go over my idea in detail.'

'Will Paul be at home?' Ashka asked.

'No. He's at school.'

Ashka smiled at Brian. 'I'd love to come.'

Paul came out of the hotel and went to Riana, who was waiting on the steps. 'The clerk said Ashka never came back,' he said dejectedly. 'He's really annoyed. She didn't pay her bill.'

'We have to keep looking.' Riana started to move away.

'Hang on,' Paul said. 'You and I can't search the whole city.'

'Alex and Katrina will help.'

'We had a bit of an argument,' Paul

admitted. 'Katrina isn't talking to me.'

'But they're your friends. They have to help.'

Paul grinned. 'Maybe when they see you, they will.'

Brian gently tucked a blanket around Christine, who was lying on the sofa. She looked pale. 'How are you feeling now?' Brian asked, stroking her forehead.

'A bit better.'

'I'm sorry I wasn't here this morning.'

A horn sounded outside the house.

'That'll be Mrs Harley,' Brian said. 'We're going to work here this afternoon.'

Brian opened the front door and saw Ashka getting out of her sports car. She held up a large teddy bear and smiled. 'The woman in the shop said that this would cheer up a sick girl.'

'Christine will love you,' Brian said. 'Come and meet her.'

He led Ashka through the house to the loungeroom. 'This is Mrs Harley,' Brian told Christine.

'Please call me Anna,' Ashka said, handing her the bear.

'I love it. Thank you, Anna.'

'I'm just sorry that it's only a toy,' Ashka said. 'I tried to find a shop that would sell me a real bear.'

Christine stared at Ashka, then decided that she was joking and laughed. Brian smiled, happy to see that his daughter liked Anna.

Paul hurried away from the school buildings to the playing field where he had left Riana. 'Alex and Katrina are stuck in class,' he said. 'I can't get them. I reckon the only sure way to stop Ashka is to tell my dad what's going on.'

'What if he doesn't believe you?' Riana asked.

'Then we'll call up Correon and get him to open the doorway. Dad can't argue with that. I'll go home and phone him. When the bell goes, find Alex and Katrina and bring them to my place.'

Riana nodded and Paul raced off.

Brian and Ashka sat in front of the computer

in the study, examining the designs for the new power suit.

'It's so wonderfully simple,' Brian explained. 'If we put magnetic power into opposing quadrants of the suit, we get lateral movement and you'll be flying.'

'How long will it take to build a suit like this?' Ashka asked.

Brian smiled. 'Not long. I've got a whole lab at my disposal.'

'Dad, Dad,' Paul yelled as he ran into the house. He passed the loungeroom and saw Christine lying on the sofa watching TV. 'What's up with you?'

'I told you I was sick,' Christine said. 'Dad had to come to school and get me. He's in his workroom ... with Mrs Harley.'

'What's she like?' Paul asked.

'Beautiful. She brought me this.' She showed Paul the teddy bear.

'Aren't you supposed to be at school?' Brian asked from the doorway.

'Yes,' Paul said guiltily, 'but ...'

'Never mind. Come up to the study. There's

someone I want you to meet.'

Grinning like a schoolboy, Brian went up the stairs. Paul followed him, curious to meet the mysterious Mrs Harley. Brian opened the study door and Paul saw a fashionably dressed woman sitting at the computer.

'Paul, this is Anna Harley,' Brian said. 'Anna, meet Paul.'

The woman swivelled her chair around from the desk. Paul stared at her in horror. It was Ashka!

A Spellbinder in the House

Ashka stood up and smiled. 'Hello, Paul. I'm so glad to meet you at last.'

'I told you she was attractive,' Brian whispered, misinterpreting the stunned look on Paul's face. 'You'll be seeing quite a bit of Anna. She and I are going to be working together ...'

'Dad, she's lying,' Paul cried. 'Her name isn't Anna. It's Ashka. She's a Spellbinder. From the parallel world. You have to get rid of her, Dad. She's evil!'

'I'm terribly sorry about this,' Brian said to Ashka, his face burning with embarrassment. 'Would you excuse us for a moment?'

Brian hustled Paul out of the study and into his bedroom. He closed the door, barely controlling his anger. 'What's going on with you? I thought all this nonsense about parallel worlds was over.'

'It's not nonsense,' Paul protested. 'Ashka's a Spellbinder!'

'Paul, stop it! Mrs Harley is an archaeologist. She's very nice. Christine thinks so too.'

'Don't let her near Christine. She's dangerous!'

'Paul, sit down. Sit down!'

Paul reluctantly sat on the bed.

'Mrs Harley is from Iceland,' Brian explained patiently. 'That's why she speaks strangely.'

'She's lying!'

'Let me finish. Anna came to me for help. She found an ancient book with details of an extraordinary technology. Designs for these incredible power suits. She even had one of the stones that powers them.'

'That's Spellbinder technology. All the Spellbinders wear power suits.'

'Stop twisting my words,' Brian said angrily.

'It's true,' Paul insisted. 'Now she wants you to build a more powerful suit so she can go back and rule Riana's world.'

'Paul, why are you doing this? Are you jealous of Anna? I'm not trying to find someone to replace your mother.'

'This has got nothing to do with Mum! Please, Dad. You've got to stop working with her.'

'No! If our research succeeds, the whole world could undergo a technological revolution. This could be the key to a cheap, non-polluting energy source. I won't have you scaring Anna off.'

'If you won't get rid of her, I will,' Paul said defiantly. Before Brian could stop him, Paul ran out of the bedroom and burst into the study.

'Get out of this house or I'll call the police,' Paul shouted at Ashka. 'I know you robbed that security van. The police will trace the money, then you'll go to gaol.'

Brian hurried in behind him. 'Paul, stop this right now! Anna, I'm sorry.'

'It's alright, Brian. If Paul doesn't want me here, I'll go.' She moved towards the door.

'Anna, wait,' Brian said. 'Why don't we go back to the laboratory? That'll give Paul time to calm down.'

'If you're sure. I don't want to bring trouble to your family.'

'I'm sure. I'll join you downstairs.'

Ashka gave Brian a warm smile as she left. Paul felt sick when his father smiled back. 'Dad, she's just using you,' he pleaded.

'That's enough,' Brian snapped. 'Stay here and look after Christine. Don't say anything about this to her. I don't want her upset. We'll talk when I get home.'

Brian went out. Paul waited until he heard the front door close, then hurried downstairs. Christine was still resting on the sofa.

'I have to go out,' Paul told her. 'Are you feeling OK?'

'I think so. Why do you have to go? I'm scared on my own.'

'You'll be alright. I'll be as quick as I can.' Paul headed for the door.

'Anna's nice, isn't she?' Christine asked. 'Dad likes her too. Maybe they'll fall in love and get married.'

'Not if I can help it,' Paul said under his breath.

Riana prowled the schoolyard during morning recess, looking for Alex and Katrina. Unable to find them, she returned to the trees by the playing fields. Paul was waiting for her.

'Ashka's at my house,' he said desperately. 'She's getting my dad to build the new power suit.'

'Didn't you tell him she's a Spellbinder?'

'Yes, but he won't listen.' Paul looked at Riana in dismay. 'I don't know how to make him believe in your world.'

'The video-camera!' Riana exclaimed. 'I brought it back with me. I recorded Ashka telling Gryvon her plan. It's in your bedroom cupboard.'

Paul smiled with relief. 'We'll take it straight to Dad's work and show him. Once he sees that and meets you, he'll have to believe me.'

They ran back to Paul's house but the front door was secured by a chain and wouldn't open. Paul rang the doorbell: there was no response. 'Christine must be asleep,' he told Riana. 'We'll go round the back.'

The back door was locked too but Riana saw that Paul's bedroom window was open. 'Why don't we climb in through there?' She started

scaling the drainpipe.

'Riana, no.'

Riana jumped down. 'Why?'

'Christine doesn't know that Ashka's a Spellbinder. I don't want to frighten her. Stay out of sight.'

Paul awkwardly clambered up the drainpipe. As he climbed across to the window, his shoes slipped. He grabbed the window ledge and hung there, his shoes scrabbling noisily on the brickwork as he pulled himself up on to the ledge. Perched there, he regained his breath, then crawled in through the window. A blanket was thrown over his head and the window slammed down on his torso, trapping him.

'Help,' Christine screamed at the top of her voice. 'Burglars! Help!'

'Christine,' Paul shouted, 'it's me!'

Christine lifted the blanket and stared at her brother in surprise. She opened the window and Paul fell into the room.

'I was scared here on my own,' Christine explained. 'I heard noises. I thought you were a burglar.'

'It's OK, sis.' Paul went to his wardrobe and

found the video-camera. 'I'm going to see Dad. Don't let anyone in the house unless it's me. Promise?'

'I promise. Why?'

'I'll tell you later,' Paul said and raced out.

Paul and Riana crouched behind a tree, out of sight of the guard hut at the entrance to Magnetronix.

'The guard knows me but he won't let you in,' Paul told Riana.

'Can't we just climb over the fence?'

'This isn't like getting into the Spellbinder's castle. There are security cameras all over the place.'

Paul saw a small truck approaching. There was a Magnetronix sign on its door.

'Quick,' Paul hissed. 'I'll distract the guard and you hop on the back of that.'

He gave the video-camera to Riana and strolled up to the gate. The guard came out of his hut. 'Hello, Paul. Here to see your dad?'

'Yeah.' Paul wiped his forehead. 'Hot, isn't it?'

'Weather report says it'll be hotter

tomorrow.' The guard opened the gate for the approaching truck. As it drove through, Paul staggered into the road in front of it. The truck screeched to a halt and the guard hurried over. 'Are you alright?'

'Yeah. I think so. I went all dizzy. It must be the heat.' Paul sat on the road and the guard and driver looked down at him.

Behind them, Riana scurried to the truck and climbed onto the tray, crouching out of sight.

'The boy's going to see his father,' the guard said to the driver. 'Why don't you give him a lift to the entrance?'

The driver opened the passenger door and Paul climbed in. The truck drove through the gate and up to the front entrance of the main building. As soon as it stopped, Riana scrambled off the back and dived into some bushes.

'Thanks,' Paul said, getting out of the cab. 'Sorry about the scare.'

The truck drove away and Paul hurried over to Riana. 'Now we have to get you past security.'

Down the side of the building, a door opened in the loading bay. A man wheeled out a large cardboard carton on a trolley. He left it by a stack of other cartons and went back inside.

Paul smiled. 'I've got an idea.'

The lift doors opened and Paul emerged, wheeling the trolley with the cardboard carton. He pushed it along the corridor past his father's office and stopped a few metres from a door which was marked 'Research Laboratory'. Paul quickly checked that the coast was clear, then lifted the carton off the trolley. Riana was hidden underneath.

Inside the laboratory, Brian held Ashka's arm as he carefully fitted a black plastic box to the wrist of the power suit.

'This is the flight control unit,' he explained. 'It regulates the direction and polarity of the suit's magnetic field.'

Ashka looked at him blankly. Brian pointed to the keypad on the top of the unit. 'Touch this button to go up and this one to go down.

Don't try and go sideways; we'll save that until we know it works.'

Ashka nodded and went inside the cage. Brian closed the door and crossed to his bank of monitoring equipment. Behind them, Paul and Riana sneaked into the laboratory and hid behind a bench. Paul noticed the old Spellbinder book on the desk beside his father.

'I'm ready,' Brian called. 'Energise the suit now.'

Ashka threw the switch on the belt of the suit. It hummed with power. Brian monitored the magnetic field strength on his computer screen. 'Good. Are you ready?'

Ashka nodded. Brian took a deep breath. 'Activate the flight control.'

Ashka touched the top button on the unit. The power hum increased. Paul and Riana watched with amazement as Ashka slowly rose off the floor of the cage.

'It works!' Brian crowed as Ashka hovered in the air. She touched the button again and slowly rose higher.

'Don't push it too far,' Brian cautioned.

Ashka ignored him and touched the button

once more. There was a crackle of electricity and smoke began to rise from the unit.

'Turn it off!' Brian yelled.

Before she could act, a shower of sparks flew from the unit and Ashka fell heavily to the floor of the cage. Brian threw the cage door open and rushed to her side. He ripped the sparking unit from her wrist and tossed it away.

'Are you alright?' he asked anxiously.

'Yes. What went wrong?'

Brian carefully picked up the still-smoking unit and turned it over. The circuit board was blackened where components had burned out. 'The circuitry overloaded. Don't worry: I can redesign it.'

'I know you can,' Ashka said. 'You have already done more than I ever hoped for. I can fly.'

She squeezed Brian's hand and smiled at him warmly. Brian glowed. This was the happiest day of his life. Paul nudged Riana and they crept out of the laboratory into the corridor.

'Now the Spellbinders will have no chance

against Ashka,' Riana said grimly to Paul.

'Don't panic. Once Dad sees what's on this, Ashka will be history.' He took the video-camera from Riana. 'Stay here until I call you.'

Paul helped Riana back under the carton and went towards the laboratory, the video-camera hidden beneath his shirt.

Brian looked up angrily as Paul came in. 'I told you to stay at home. You're supposed to be looking after your sister.'

'I came to apologise,' Paul explained. He went to Ashka. 'Mrs Harley, I'm sorry about how I behaved.' Ashka looked at him warily. 'I don't know what I was thinking,' Paul said contritely. 'It won't happen again.'

Brian smiled. 'Well, I'm glad that's sorted out.'

'Dad, could I ask you a couple of questions while I'm here?' Paul asked.

'Ask away.'

'It's ... a bit embarrassing. It's about a girl. Could we go to your office?'

'Excuse me a moment, Anna,' Brian said to Ashka. 'Time for a little father-and-son chat.' He put his arm around Paul and led him towards the door. Ashka watched suspiciously as they went out.

'Now, Paul, you don't have to be embarrassed,' Brian said as they headed along the corridor. 'Girls are people too.' Riana watched them pass, through eyeholes she had made in the side of the carton.

Brian closed the door of his office and gave Paul a fatherly smile. 'OK, son. What's on your mind? Ask me anything you like.'

Paul took the video-camera from under his shirt and began plugging it into Brian's TV. 'I can prove Ashka's from the parallel world.'

Anger flared in Brian's eyes. 'Paul!'

'She's on this tape, explaining her plan. Riana videoed her.'

'Riana?' Brian said scathingly. 'Your imaginary girlfriend from the parallel world?'

'She's not imaginary. She's outside.'

'With Superman, I suppose?'

'Just watch the tape, Dad. If it doesn't convince you, I promise I'll never mention any of this stuff again.'

Brian grudgingly nodded and Paul pressed the play button on the camera. Gryvon appeared on the TV screen. He was in the vault beneath the ruined castle, holding the old Spellbinder book.

'Who's that?' Brian asked.

'Gryvon. He's Ashka's Apprentice. Don't you recognise the book?'

As Brian moved towards the screen for a closer look, the picture started to break up. 'I can't see anything. The tape must be faulty.'

Paul looked up in fear as the lights in the room started to flicker. 'It's not the tape, it's Ashka! She's using the power suit to interfere with the tape.'

Brian turned off the TV. 'Paul, sit down. I'm going to call a doctor.'

'I don't need a doctor,' Paul shouted.

Ashka stood listening outside the office door. Satisfied that she had prevented Paul from exposing her, she turned off the power suit and headed back towards the laboratory. She was surprised to see a large cardboard carton charging towards her. They collided and crashed to the floor.

Riana wriggled out of the carton and started

to run towards Brian's office. Ashka energised the suit and pointed at a piece of abstract metal art standing in the corridor. The suit's magnetic field attracted it, pulling the sculpture over. It fell onto Riana, knocking her out.

Inside the office, Paul fought to get past Brian. 'Dad, you've got to believe me!'

'Sit down and I'll listen to you.'

Paul stopped struggling and Brian let him go. As soon as Brian relaxed, Paul bolted for the door. He threw it open and raced out.

'Riana!' Paul shouted. There was no reply.

Brian came out of the office.

'Riana was in that box,' Paul said desperately, pointing to the carton lying on its side. He raced down the corridor and into the laboratory. Brian chased after him. There was no sign of Ashka.

'Anna?' Brian called.

'Her name's Ashka,' Paul said. 'She's not here. And the power suit's gone.'

Brian realised that the Spellbinder book was missing as well and turned angrily on Paul. 'If you've made her take this discovery to some other lab ...'

'Dad, she's got Riana!'

'Paul, pull yourself together.' Brian took Paul's arm but Paul twisted free and ran out of the laboratory.

Paul raced into the stairwell and took the steps two at a time. He burst out of the building and had to leap aside as Ashka roared past in her sports car. A piece of blue fabric was sticking out of the boot. Paul realised it was Riana's denim jacket.

Brian ran out of the building and saw Paul chasing Ashka's car. 'Paul! Anna!' he yelled but neither of them stopped.

The guard opened the gate as Ashka approached.

'Close the gate!' Paul shouted. 'Stop her!'

The guard looked round and Ashka drove through and accelerated away. Paul cried out with frustration. Brian ran up to him, panting.

'Riana's in the boot,' Paul said. 'I saw her jacket.'

'What's all the fuss, Mr Reynolds?' the guard asked.

'Ted, did my son come in today with a girl? Think carefully.'

'Nope. He was on his own.'

'He didn't see her because I distracted his attention,' Paul explained.

'He was acting pretty strangely,' the guard told Brian.

Brian took Paul's arm and led him towards the carpark. 'Paul,' he said gently, 'I think you might be ... still suffering some after-effects from when you were lost in the bush. The mind can play funny tricks.'

'Ashka's kidnapped Riana,' Paul protested. 'You've got to call the police.'

'What I'm going to do is take you home,' Brian said firmly. 'Then I'm calling a doctor.'

Ashka turned off the street into the driveway of a large, old house. The garden was overgrown and the windows boarded up. Ashka got out of the car and unlocked the front door. Making sure that no-one was watching, she went back to the car and opened the boot. She lifted out Riana's unconscious body and carried it inside.

Some time later, Riana's eyes opened and she looked around. She was sitting in a chair in a dingy attic room. Ashka was standing in front of her. Riana tried to get up and realised her hands and feet were tied to the chair.

'Where am I?' Riana asked.

'Where no-one can find you. Don't cause me any trouble, or Paul and his family will suffer.'

Ashka bound a piece of cloth securely over Riana's mouth, then went out and shut the door. Riana heard the sound of a bolt sliding home, then footsteps walking down stairs. She tried to cry out, but the gag muffled her shouts. She struggled with the ropes, but they were tightly tied and she could barely move. There was nothing she could do.

'Why would I lie to you about all this?' Paul asked as Brian parked the car in the drive of their house.

'I don't think you're lying. I think you believe what you're saying but what you're saying doesn't make any sense.' Brian got out and headed for the front door. 'Now I don't want you upsetting your sister with all this.'

'So you think I'm crazy?' Paul said angrily as he followed Brian inside.

'What's going on, Dad?' Christine called.

'Nothing, sweetheart. How are you feeling?' Brian went into the loungeroom where Christine was lying on the sofa.

'Dad,' Paul pleaded, 'you have to go back and look at the tape!'

The phone rang. Brian picked it up. 'Yes? Anna!'

'Ask her where Riana is!' Paul yelled.

Brian glared at him. 'Where are you, Anna? Why did you leave so suddenly?'

'I thought you needed some time with Paul,' Ashka replied. 'I hope you aren't angry with me?'

'Of course I'm not.'

'When can we start work again?'

'Why don't you bring the suit here?' Brian suggested. 'I've got everything I need to repair the flight control unit.'

'That's sounds wonderful.'

Brian smiled. 'Great. See you soon.' He hung up.

'Don't let her back in the house,' Paul begged. 'Please!'

'What's going on?' Christine asked anxiously.

'Go and lie down, Paul,' Brian ordered. 'Now!'

Paul didn't move. Brian picked up the phone and started to dial.

'Why don't you ask to see her driver's licence?' Paul asked stubbornly. 'Or her credit cards? I'll bet she doesn't have any. She won't even know what they are. Just ask her.'

Brian turned away and spoke into the phone. 'Could I speak to Dr Marsden? It's about my son.'

Paul ran out of the room. The front door slammed.

Paul hammered on Alex's front door until Nick opened it.

'I've got to see Alex,' Paul insisted.

'Sorry, man. He went to work with Pop. He had one of those detector things. Reckoned he was worried about how much electro-moronic radiation the old man was getting ...'

Nick stared in surprise as Paul bolted away.

It was dusk and floodlights were starting to come on in the container terminal. Alex sat with his father in the cramped cab of the crane. He was holding one of the magnetometers he and Paul had made.

'How can the electro-magnets affect me?' Stavros asked. 'I'm not made of metal.'

'Their magnetic field affects your brain,' Alex explained. 'If it's too strong, it might make you stupid.'

His father chuckled. 'Your mother would say it's too late.'

'Turn them on and I'll see how strong the field is up here,' Alex said.

Stavros flicked a switch on his control panel and there was a loud electrical hum as the electro-magnets energised. Alex heard a hiss and turned. He was surprised to see Paul standing in the cab doorway. Paul put a finger over his lips, pointed downwards then disappeared.

'Dad, I'll be back in a sec,' Alex said. 'I ...

want to check the field strength closer to the magnet.'

Alex left the cab and climbed down to where Paul was waiting on the ground. 'What are you doing here?'

'Ashka's getting my dad to build her a new power suit,' Paul said desperately. 'I think he's falling in love with her. And she's kidnapped Riana.'

'Riana?' Alex echoed in amazement. 'But she went home. Paul, you're not making sense.'

'We've got to find Riana and rescue her.' Paul grabbed Alex's arm but Alex pulled away.

'The adventure's over, mate. Let it go. You've got to get back to normal.'

'Paul,' Stavros yelled from the crane cab, 'this is a restricted area. I had to get special permission for Alex to be here.'

'Please come with me,' Paul begged.

'Sorry, man, I'm busy.' Alex started to climb back up the ladder.

Katrina looked sceptically at Paul, who was standing on the porch outside her front door. **309**

'Where's your proof?'

'Why would I make this up?' Paul said impatiently.

'Because you're jealous of Alex spending time with me.'

'Don't be stupid!' Paul shouted.

'Katrina, who are you talking to?' Mrs Muggleton called from inside the house.

'No-one, Mum.' Katrina closed the door in Paul's face.

Paul trudged towards his house, racking his brains for some way to thwart Ashka. He was dismayed to see her car parked in the driveway. The sound of laughter came from inside the house and Paul looked up. Through the study window, he could see Brian and Ashka standing close together.

Paul quietly entered the house and crept up the stairs. The study door was open and Paul could see Ashka standing by the workbench, watching intently as Brian assembled the new flight control unit that would fit on the wrist of the power suit. The power suit itself was draped over a chair near the door. Without it,

Ashka would be helpless. Paul tiptoed into the room.

'If this works,' Brian said gleefully, 'cars will become obsolete overnight. No-one will want to drive when they can fly. The oil companies will scream blue murder. You're going to be rich beyond belief.'

'No, Brian,' Ashka corrected. '*We're* going to be rich. I could never have done this without you.'

Paul felt sick as he saw his father smile at Ashka like a lovesick puppy. He swallowed his anger, carefully lifted the power suit off the chair and sneaked out. As Paul hurried away from the study, Christine came bounding up the stairs.

'Where have you been?' she asked loudly. 'What's that?' She pointed at the power suit.

Paul hushed her, but it was too late: Brian and Ashka came out of the study and saw Paul with the suit.

'Bring that back,' Brian ordered.

Paul started to push past Christine but Ashka lunged forward and seized the arm of the suit. Paul tried to pull it free but Brian grabbed him and forced him to let it go.

Paul glared at Ashka. 'What have you done with Riana?'

Ashka looked at him blankly. 'I don't know what you're talking about.'

'You're a liar!'

'Paul, stop this!' Brian shouted. Paul glared defiantly at his father.

'Don't fight,' Christine pleaded, close to tears.

'You're upsetting your sister,' Brian said sharply.

Ashka put her arm around Christine and smiled. 'Don't worry, everything will be alright.'

Paul stormed into his bedroom and slammed the door.

Paul lay on his bed, staring at the wall and feeling utterly helpless. The door opened and the light went on. Paul rolled over and saw Ashka standing in the doorway. She closed the door and moved towards him.

'What do you want?' Paul asked, trying to keep the fear from his voice.

'Your cooperation.'

'Drop dead, Ashka.'

He turned away but Ashka sat on the bed beside him. 'I just want the power suit to be finished,' she said sweetly. 'Then I'll take it back to my world and you'll never see me again.'

'What about Riana?' Paul asked.

'She's quite safe. Whether she remains that way depends on you. The same goes for your father and your sister.' Ashka's voice hardened. 'Don't cross me again, Paul.'

There was a tap on the door, and Brian came in. He was surprised to see Ashka. 'Anna? What are you doing in here?'

'I heard something and came to see what it was. Paul was having a nightmare.' Ashka patted Paul's hand. 'But you're alright now, aren't you, Paul?'

Paul reluctantly nodded.

'I enjoyed our little chat,' Ashka said. She got off the bed and joined Brian.

'Goodnight, Paul,' Brian said, relieved that his son seemed to be accepting Ashka at last. He went out.

Ashka flashed Paul a triumphant smile and then switched out the light. As soon as she was gone, Paul leaped out of bed and shut the door. He dragged his chest of drawers in front of it to keep it closed and then sank to the floor, trembling. He'd never been so scared in his life.

Breakfast of Champions

Paul huddled under his doona in the corner of his bedroom. He felt wretched. Ashka had won. His head jerked around as the door handle turned. The door opened, but stopped against the chest of drawers barricading it.

'Paul?' Brian called from the corridor.

'Go away,' Paul croaked.

'You've got to come and see this,' Brian said excitedly. 'It's very important.'

Paul reluctantly got up and pulled the chest away from the door. He followed his father into the study and was dismayed to see Ashka with her arm around Christine.

'You're not going to believe this,' Christine said excitedly. 'Dad's invented a flying suit.'

Brian pointed proudly to the power suit on the workbench. 'This is the project I was telling you about. It's going to be the biggest thing since the invention of the motor car.'

'Aren't you pleased for your father?' Ashka asked. Paul didn't reply. Ashka stepped forward and whispered in his ear. 'Be patient. This will all be over soon. Then I'll let Riana go.'

Paul forced a smile. 'That's terrific, Dad.'

Brian took a Polaroid camera from the bench. 'Anna, come here and let Christine take a photo.'

'I want to try the suit,' Ashka said.

'Sorry. Until we know the strength of the magnetic field, we can't risk using it outside the lab.'

Ashka moved to Brian's side. Brian handed the camera to Christine and she took aim. 'Smile.' Ashka jumped as the camera flashed. A photo emerged from the slot.

'Now can we go?' Ashka asked impatiently. She picked up the power suit and headed for the door. Paul tensed, ready to grab the suit and make a run for it.

'Wait,' Christine said. 'If this is such an important day, we should celebrate. Paul and I will make you both a special breakfast.'

'I'm not hungry,' Ashka said.

'Anna, we've been working all night,' Brian reminded her. 'I'm starving. Thank you, Christine, that's a lovely idea.'

Ashka forced a smile and put the suit down. Christine put the camera on the workbench and pulled Paul out of the room.

Christine opened the refrigerator and peered at the contents. 'What do you think Anna likes to eat?' she asked Paul.

'How about deep-fried cow dung?'

'Yuk! That's sick.'

'I'd like to make her sick,' Paul said angrily under his breath. That gave him an idea. 'What about scrambled eggs?'

'Great.' Christine started taking the eggs from the fridge.

'You make a start,' Paul said, 'I'll be right back.' He hurried upstairs to the bathroom. In the cabinet was a bottle of liquid laxative. Paul pocketed the bottle and went back to the kitchen.

The dining table was meticulously set for four.

There was even a vase of flowers in the centre of the table-cloth. Paul came in from the kitchen with a frying pan. He dished out scrambled eggs onto three plates and was about to get out the bottle of laxative when Christine came in with a pot of coffee.

'We forgot the juice,' Paul told her.

Christine put the pot on the table and went back to the kitchen. Paul quickly opened the bottle, poured a generous dose of laxative into the pan and slipped the bottle back in his pocket. He stirred the laxative into the remaining eggs, then scooped them onto the fourth plate. He took a flower from the vase and placed it on top of the eggs. 'This plate's for Anna,' he said as Christine came back with the tray of orange juices.

Christine went to the bottom of the stairs. 'Breakfast is served,' she yelled.

Paul quickly pulled out the bottle and poured more laxative into a glass of orange juice which he put by Ashka's plate. He slid the bottle back in his pocket just as Brian and Ashka came in.

'This looks wonderful,' Brian said. He pulled

out a chair. 'Anna, you sit here.'

'No,' Christine cried. 'That's Anna's plate with the flower on it.'

'It looks lovely,' Ashka said and sat down.

As they began to eat, Paul watched Ashka anxiously. She didn't seem quite sure about the taste of the eggs and washed them down with a big gulp of orange juice. Paul smiled to himself. Ashka quickly finished her breakfast and waited impatiently as Brian ate some toast and marmalade. Paul kept stealing glances at her. She was definitely beginning to look queasy.

'If the flying suit works,' Christine asked her father, 'will you and Anna be famous?'

'Once we demonstrate it, we'll be on the cover of every newspaper in the world,' Brian said confidently. 'We might even win the Nobel prize, eh Anna?'

Ashka belched loudly.

'What did you think of the scrambled eggs, Anna?' Christine asked.

'I've never tasted eggs quite like them.' Ashka suddenly got up, holding her stomach. 'Where is the ... outhouse?'

'I think she means toilet,' Paul said.

'Through there,' Brian said, pointing. 'Are you alright?'

Ashka ran out, clutching her stomach and groaning. Brian got up and went after her. Christine anxiously watched them go.

'Don't worry,' Paul told her, 'I'm sure it wasn't your cooking.'

Christine began to clear the table. Paul headed for the stairs. This was his chance to destroy the power suit.

Paul opened the study window. He lifted the power suit off the bench but before he could throw it out, Brian came in. 'What are you doing?' he asked suspiciously

'Er ... I was just having a look at the flying suit,' Paul said quickly. 'It's amazing. How's Anna?'

'Bit of a nasty stomach. I'm sure she'll be fine.' Brian took the suit from Paul and started to pack it into a bag.

'Dad, what makes the suit fly?' Paul asked, playing for time.

'The suit generates a powerful force which

repels the earth's magnetic field.' Brian showed Paul the flight control unit on the wrist of the suit. 'This controls the direction of the force. Anna and I were up all night rebuilding it. The first version burnt out.' He picked up the old unit from the workbench and pointed to the charred circuitry on its underside.

'Was that Anna calling?' Paul suddenly asked.

Brian put the bag down and hurried out. Paul quickly detached the flight control unit from the wrist of the suit and swapped it for the burnt-out one. He dropped the new unit into the waste bin under the bench just as Brian came back.

'It wasn't Anna,' Brian said. 'Look, it's getting late. Can you take Christine to school while I look after Anna?'

Paul nodded. Brian zipped up the bag and carried it out. As Paul followed, he noticed the Polaroid photo on the bench. He slid it into his pocket.

'I've got to see Alex,' Paul said, once he and

Christine were outside the house. 'You can get to school on your own.'

'But I don't feel well again,' Christine complained. 'I don't want to go to school.'

'Christine, just go,' Paul said impatiently.

She walked off, looking miserable. Paul ran the other way.

'Ohms are a measurement of what?' Katrina asked, looking up from her science textbook. Alex was nervously pacing the garage. He surreptitiously pulled up his shirt sleeve and glanced at his arm. 'Electrical resistance.'

'Correct. What is a kilojoule?'

Alex looked at his arm again. Katrina grabbed him and pushed up his sleeve. Words were scribbled all over his arm.

'Alex, you've studied for this test,' Katrina said angrily. 'You don't need to cheat.'

'I just don't want to fail any more,' Alex protested.

'You won't. Come on, we have to go.' Katrina headed for the door.

As Alex picked up his bag, he noticed the two-way radios on the workbench. 'I'd better give these back to Nathan. We won't be needing them any more.' He was putting them in his bag when Paul burst in.

'Ashka's at my house now,' he panted. 'Dad's finished her new power suit.'

'We went through this last night, Paul,' Katrina said irritably. 'Where's your proof?'

Paul took out the Polaroid photo and slammed it on the bench. 'Will that do?'

Alex and Katrina stared at the picture of Brian, Ashka and the power suit.

'I need you to convince my dad that I'm telling the truth,' Paul pleaded. 'Come with me? Please?'

Brian opened the sports car door and Ashka groaned as she settled slowly into the driver's seat.

'Are you sure you wouldn't be better resting?' Brian asked.

'I'm too excited. I have to see if the suit flies. I'll go home and change and meet you at the laboratory.'

'This is going to be a day we'll never forget,' Brian said, grinning. Ashka smiled back weakly, then started the car and drove away.

Brian put the bag containing the power suit into his car. He was reversing out of the drive when Paul, Alex and Katrina came running up the street.

'Dad,' Paul yelled, 'wait!'

Brian didn't hear and drove away.

'Now what are we going to do?' Alex asked.

'We've got to find out where Ashka is staying,' Paul replied. 'That must be where she's got Riana.'

In the study, Paul found his father's address book. He flipped through it and found the entry for Anna Harley.

'Ashka's address isn't here,' he said with dismay.

'She didn't want your dad turning up unexpectedly and finding Riana,' Katrina suggested.

Alex looked at the address book. 'Her mobile phone number's here.'

'That's no use,' Paul said.

Alex smiled: 'Leave it to the master.' He checked the phone book, then picked up the phone and dialled. 'Hi. My name's Harley.

I've just bought one of your mobile phones. Great little unit. But I've just moved and I want to make sure you've got the right address to send the bill to ... My phone number is 018 000 666 ... 84 McNab Street. That's the one.' He hung up and grinned. 'What are we waiting for?'

As they turned to go, Christine appeared in the doorway.

'What are you doing here?' Paul asked. 'You're supposed to be at school.'

'I feel awful,' she moaned. 'I want to stay at home.'

Paul controlled his frustration. 'Alright, you can stay. Go and watch TV.'

Christine went downstairs. Paul looked at the address that Alex had written down. 'Let's go and find Riana.'

Paul, Alex and Katrina stood on McNab street, looking at the large old house.

'This is it,' Paul said, checking the address.

'Are you sure?' Katrina asked. 'It looks deserted.'

Paul was about to open the gate when he

saw Ashka's red sports car parked down the driveway. 'She's here! Get back.' He pulled Alex and Katrina out of sight behind a tree.

'What are you worried about?' Alex asked. 'There are three of us and only one of her.'

'What if she's got a guard dog?' Katrina replied. 'Or a gun? Or the power suit?'

Alex shuddered. 'Good point.'

'So how can we get inside?' Paul asked.

'Ashka's from another world,' Katrina pointed out. 'She doesn't know how our world works. She can't even read.'

Alex looked puzzled. 'So?'

'So we just have to think of a way to trick her into letting one of us inside.'

'Who's going to go?' Alex asked.

'You,' Paul said. 'You're the only one of us that Ashka doesn't know.'

Alex groaned.

Armed with a school folder and pen, Alex strode up the path to the front door. He took a deep breath and rang the bell. He beamed as Ashka opened the door.

'Good morning, madam. I'm from the gas

company. We've had a report of a leak in the area so I'm here to check your pipes.'

'I'm busy. Go away.' Ashka tried to close the door but Alex put his foot in the way.

'Madam, if there is a leak, your house could fill up with gas and explode.'

'Come back tomorrow,' Ashka said.

'Sorry. I have to do it today. Here's my authorisation.'

Alex opened his wallet and took out a video rental card. Ashka peered at it, wishing she could read the writing of this world. Not wanting to draw attention to herself, she reluctantly let Alex in. He looked around the dusty hallway and sniffed.

'Mmm. I can definitely smell something. In a house this old, there'll be pipes everywhere. I'll have to check all the rooms.'

'I have to go out,' Ashka protested.

'Shouldn't take too long.' Before Ashka could argue, Alex nipped into the closest room, sniffing loudly.

In the attic, Riana was struggling with the ropes tying her to the chair when she heard a familiar voice.

'Gas leaks can be tricky to find,' Alex said. 'You've got to have the nose for it.'

Riana tried to shout but the gag muffled her cries. She looked desperately around. An old bottle was standing close to the edge of a rickety table. Riana edged the chair across the floor and kicked the table: the bottle teetered.

'They used to use dogs for this job,' Alex said, sniffing his way around an empty room. 'But they just couldn't fill out the report forms when they got back to the office.' He laughed at his joke. Ashka didn't.

'Are you going to be much longer?' she asked.

There was the sound of breaking glass from above their heads. Alex looked up eagerly. 'What was that?'

'Rats. The house is full of them.'

Alex sniffed vigorously. 'I think there's some gas in here. You should let some air in.' He went to a window and undid the catch.

Before Alex could open it, Ashka grabbed his arm and propelled him towards the door.

'That's enough,' she said, hustling him into the corridor.

Alex noticed a staircase at the end of the passage. 'I'll just have a look up there.'

'You can't,' Ashka said, 'the stairs are rotten.' She pushed Alex to the front door and shoved him outside.

'Thanks for your cooperation,' Alex said. 'Have a nice ...' The door slammed in his face. He breathed a sigh of relief and went to the gate. Paul and Katrina hurried up to him.

'Don't ask me to do anything like that again,' Alex said.

'Any sign of Riana?' Paul asked.

'I think she's there. I heard something smash upstairs and Ashka's very nervy.'

'Any alarms?' Katrina asked.

'Not that I could see.'

'We'll wait until she's gone, then break in,' Paul decided.

'You don't have to break anything,' Alex said proudly. 'I unlocked a window.'

Riana was struggling with her ropes when the attic door opened and Ashka came in. She saw

329

the broken bottle on the floor.

'It's no use, Riana. No-one's coming to help you.'

Ashka's mobile phone rang and she took it from her pocket. 'Yes? ... Brian, how nice of you to call ... I'm fine now ... Good. I'll see you at the laboratory very soon.'

Ashka put the phone away and smiled at Riana. 'My new power suit is ready. Once I control the Spellbinders, my first task will be to banish your family to the Wastelands.'

Riana thrashed helplessly in the chair. Ashka laughed and went out, slamming the door. Then came the sound of the bolt sliding home.

Paul, Alex and Katrina watched from hiding as Ashka came out of the house, carrying the old Spellbinder book. She got into her car and drove away. Once she was gone, they hurried through the gate and went around the back of the house. An elderly woman watched suspiciously from the window of a house across the road.

Alex led the way to the ground-floor

window and was about to climb in when Paul stopped him. 'It's my turn. You two go out front and keep watch.'

Alex took one of the two-way radios from his bag and gave it to Paul. 'Keep in touch,' he said as he followed Katrina towards the front of the house.

Paul climbed through the window. Following Alex's instructions, he moved warily through the dingy house. He found the staircase and carefully climbed it, the boards creaking under his feet. The door at the top was bolted and secured with a padlock. Paul put his mouth close to the door. 'Riana?'

From behind the door came a muffled cry, then a thumping on the floor. 'It's OK,' Paul called back, 'I'm coming.'

Paul inspected the heavy padlock. There was no way he could prise it open. He took out his Swiss Army knife and used the blade to start undoing the screws that held the bolt to the door. They came out easily and he was starting on the last screw when Alex's worried voice came from the two-way radio: 'Paul, there's a police car coming.'

'I've found Riana but I need time to get her out,' Paul said into his radio. 'Can you distract them?'

'You owe me bigtime, pal.'

Paul smiled grimly and continued turning the screw. It came out and the bolt dropped to the floor. Paul threw the attic door open. He hurried to Riana and removed the gag. 'Are you OK?'

'Yes, but Ashka's gone to your father's laboratory. We have to stop her.'

Paul started cutting through Riana's ropes.

The elderly woman watched smugly from across the road as a young policeman and a policewoman got out of their car and walked towards Ashka's house. Alex and Katrina were searching through the overgrown garden.

'Here, Warren. Here, boy,' Alex called.

'What are you two doing?' the policewoman called.

'Looking for a dog, Officer,' Alex answered politely, coming over with Katrina. 'His name's Warren.'

'Isn't that a better name for a rabbit?' the

policeman asked, sniggering.

'I really miss him,' Katrina said sadly. 'Warren was a mangy old stray with one leg and most of his teeth missing. I nursed him back to health.'

'Sounds like you should have had him put down,' the policeman said with a smirk.

'Ralph!' the policewoman said sharply. She turned to Alex and Katrina. 'There's no sign of him here. Shouldn't you be getting to school?'

Alex looked at his watch. 'Oh no!' he said in mock dismay. 'We're going to be late for our test.'

'We'll give you a lift,' the policewoman said.

Paul and Riana scrambled over the back fence of Ashka's house and ran along the lane at the rear. It led to a busy road. Paul saw a taxi approaching and flagged it down.

'We want to go to Magnetronix,' Paul told the driver as they got in. 'It's an emergency. I know the way.'

The journey seemed to take forever, but they finally neared the Magnetronix buildings.

'We have to get Dad to look at the videotape,' Paul whispered to Riana. 'As soon as we get inside, you go to the office. I'll find a way to get him away from Ashka.'

The taxi stopped at the gate.

'Get on the floor,' Paul hissed. Riana quickly crouched on the floor of the taxi as the guard came over.

'Hi, Ted,' Paul called out of his window. 'I'm here to see my dad.'

'You're here so often, you should be on the payroll,' the guard joked. Paul laughed and the guard waved the taxi through.

It pulled up outside the main entrance and the driver checked the meter. 'That'll be $19.60.'

'Sorry,' Paul said. 'I haven't got any money.' The driver glared at him. 'Don't worry. I'll get my dad to pay. I'll be right back.' He opened the door.

'I've heard that before,' the driver snapped, getting out too. 'I'm coming with you.' He followed Paul towards the entrance. 'Your dad had better be in there, son, or you're in big trouble.'

They went through the doors. Riana got out of the taxi and sneaked after them.

Dressed in the power suit, Ashka stood inside the Faraday cage, jabbing at the buttons on the flight control unit. Nothing was happening.

'Why won't it fly?' she angrily asked Brian. 'You said I'd be able to fly!' She thumped the unit with her fist.

'That won't help,' Brian said. 'Come out and let me have a look.'

Brian opened the cage door and Ashka emerged. Brian removed the unit from her wrist and was surprised to see that the back was blackened. 'This is the unit that burnt out.'

'Then why did you use it?' Ashka demanded.

'I didn't.' Brian thought for a moment. 'While you were ill, I found Paul in my study. He must have swapped them. Why would he do that?' He looked around as the laboratory door opened and Paul came in with the taxi-driver.

'Is this your son?' the driver asked Brian.

'Yes. Paul, what are you doing here?'

'He took a taxi ride he can't pay for,' the driver said. 'You owe me twenty bucks.'

Ashka pushed the driver aside and glared at Paul. 'What have you done with the flight control unit?'

'Take it easy, Anna,' Brian said. 'Paul, did you interfere with the suit?'

'Hey, what about me?' the driver demanded.

'Nobody cares about you,' Ashka snapped. 'Be quiet. Paul?'

'I'll be quiet when I get my money,' the driver said loudly.

'Look, just wait for a minute,' Brian asked. 'Paul, I want an answer.'

'Listen, Einstein,' the driver bellowed, 'while you're standing here arguing, I'm losing money. Where's my twenty-five bucks?'

'Twenty-five?' Paul exclaimed. 'Dad, he's trying to rip you off!'

'Paul!' Brian roared. 'Go and wait in my office!'

Paul went out, only too happy to comply.

'I'm sorry about this,' Brian told the driver. 'I'll go and get my wallet. Wait here.'

Brian left the laboratory and hurried into his office. He shut the door. 'Paul, what's going on with you? I've never ...' He stopped.

Paul was standing by the TV. The video-camera was plugged into it and Ashka was on the screen, talking to Gryvon in the vault under the ruined castle. She was holding the old Spellbinder book.

'I'll take this to Paul's world,' Ashka was telling Gryvon. 'Their scientists will be able to improve these designs with their computers. When I come back, no-one will be able to stand against me. I'll rule the Spellbinders.'

Paul paused the tape and looked at his father. 'This is what I was trying to show you. That woman in the lab is called Ashka. She's from the parallel world. Riana?'

Brian stared in bewilderment as Riana stood up from her hiding place behind his desk.

'Hello, Brian,' she said. 'I know it is hard for you to believe but I do come from the Spellbinders' land.'

'This can't be happening,' Brian said, dumbfounded.

'It is,' Paul said. 'You have to listen to us.'

'In my world, the Spellbinders use the power suits to control us,' Riana explained. 'And now you've built one that Ashka can use to take over the Spellbinders.'

'She'll control their whole world,' Paul said. 'No-one will be able to stand up to her. She'll be a dictator.'

As Brian grappled with these revelations, the door opened and Ashka came in. 'Riana?' she gasped.

'See, Dad?' Paul said quickly. 'She knows who Riana is.'

'Brian, your son's not well,' Ashka said. 'Neither is the girl. I can explain.'

'Yeah?' Paul asked. 'Explain that.' He pointed to the TV.

As Ashka turned to look at the screen, Paul made a grab for the powerstone on the belt of the power suit. Ashka knocked him away. Before Riana could move, Ashka energised the power suit. A glowing ball of energy appeared in her hand and she pointed at Paul. 'Tell me where the control unit is!'

Brian stepped between them. 'Don't threaten my son! Now take off the suit or I'll call Security.'

He reached for the phone but Ashka hurled the bolt and the phone exploded. Another ball of energy appeared in her hand. She aimed it at Brian.

'Tell me where the unit is,' she yelled at Paul, 'or your father will suffer!'

Flight

Paul looked desperately from his father to Riana. If he told Ashka where the flight control unit was, it would save his father's life but Riana's whole world would suffer.

Ashka raised her hand towards Brian, ready to hurl the power-bolt. 'Tell me where it is!'

The door slammed open and the angry taxi-driver stormed into the office. 'Where's my money?'

As Ashka whirled around, Brian grabbed his computer monitor and pushed it towards her. The heavy monitor, mounted on a swivelling arm, swung round and hit Ashka in the back, knocking her over.

'Oi!' the taxi-driver yelled, 'that's no way to treat a lady.'

Brian, Paul and Riana pushed past him and raced out of the office. The driver bent to help

Ashka up but she shrugged him off. 'Don't touch me, you ignorant pile of ox dung!'

'This is incredible,' Brian exclaimed as he hurried Paul and Riana towards the fire escape. 'There really is a parallel universe.'

'That's what I've been trying to tell you,' Paul said.

'I should have believed you. I'm sorry.'

Behind them, Ashka burst out of the office. Brian looked over his shoulder and saw her energise the power suit. He pushed Paul and Riana through the doorway of a storeroom as Ashka fired her bolt. Brian dived to the floor and it flew over him, exploding against a wall. Paul and Riana grabbed Brian's arms and pulled him through the door.

Brian pushed Paul and Riana towards an exit at the rear of the storeroom. 'Go and call Security.'

'What about you?' Paul asked.

Brian jammed a broomstick through the door handle to hold it shut. 'Go!'

As Riana followed Paul towards the exit, she noticed a metal bucket lying in a sink of water.

341

'Look!' She picked up the bucket.

Paul got the idea, and lifted another bucket from a shelf. They began to fill them with water.

'Paul,' Brian hissed, 'get out!'

'No, Dad. We can use water to short out the suit. We did it before in Riana's world.'

'But ...'

Before Brian could finish, the door exploded inwards and he was thrown across the room. Ashka strode through the smoking doorway. Paul and Riana raced forward and hurled their buckets of water over her. To their dismay, Ashka energised the power suit.

'I waterproofed the circuits,' Brian croaked from the floor.

Riana lifted the bucket to hit Ashka but she stepped back and switched a control on the power suit belt. The suit's magnetic field activated and the bucket flew out of Riana's hand and into Ashka's.

Paul threw his bucket. The force of the throw was multiplied by the attraction of the power suit's magnetic field, and Ashka staggered as the heavy bucket hit her. Paul pulled a bundle of metal rods off a shelf and threw them. They stuck to the power suit; Ashka tottered under their weight. Paul, Brian and Riana grabbed every metal object they could find and hurled them at Ashka. She collapsed under the weight of the metal stuck to the suit and lay still.

Brian cautiously examined her. 'She's out cold. Good thinking, Paul.'

'Let's get the suit off her,' Riana said. She reached for the buckles.

'What *did* you do with the good control unit?' Brian asked Paul.

'It's in the waste bin in your study.'

Ashka's hand suddenly moved the switch on the suit belt and the magnetic field went off. The metal objects dropped away as Ashka started to get up.

'Run!' Brian yelled.

They raced out of the storeroom and along the corridor to the lifts. Brian jabbed the call button and was relieved when the lift door opened immediately. He bundled Paul and Riana in ahead of him and punched the down button. The door closed and the lift started to descend.

'Ashka heard where the flight unit is,' Riana said. 'She'll go after it.'

'We have to get there before her,' Brian said.

'Oh no,' Paul groaned, 'Christine's at home.'

Brian paled. 'What?!'

'She was feeling sick again so I ...'

Before Paul could finish, the ceiling light started flickering and the lift stopped.

'What's happening?' Riana asked anxiously.

They felt the lift start to rise.

'Ashka's taking us back up,' Paul cried. 'Dad, do something!'

Brian hit the emergency stop button but it had no effect. He grabbed the telephone. 'This is Brian Reynolds. I need help!' There was no answer.

Ashka stood by the lift door, directing energy from the power suit to the call button. There was a 'ping' as the lift arrived and the door opened.

'Out,' she barked. Brian, Paul and Riana filed out of the lift and Ashka herded them into the laboratory. She pointed to the Faraday cage. 'In there.'

Once Paul, Riana and Brian were inside the cage, Ashka slammed the door and melted the lock with a power-bolt.

'What are you going to do?' Brian asked.

'Destroy all traces of our work,' Ashka replied coldly. 'No-one else must have my power.'

She energised the suit and fired bolt after bolt at Brian's computers. They exploded in balls of flame. Ashka picked up the old Spellbinder book and threw it into the fire. The ancient pages ignited instantly. A fire alarm started wailing and Ashka quickly silenced it with another bolt. The explosion severed an electrical conduit running up the laboratory wall. A thick electrical cable dropped towards the top of the cage, sparks flying from its exposed wires.

'Get off the floor,' Brian yelled.

Paul, Riana and Brian scrambled onto a wooden table just as the cable touched the cage, showering them with sparks. Riana shrank back towards the cage wall. Paul grabbed her.

'Don't touch the metal or you'll die.' He

kicked a spanner off the table. Sparks flew as it hit the electrified floor of the cage.

'You can't leave us here,' Brian begged as Ashka went towards the door.

'I am a Spellbinder. I can do what I like.' She strode out.

'Help!' Brian and Paul shouted. 'Help us!' No-one came.

Riana reached carefully down from the table and picked up a wooden stool. She swung it hard against the cage wall but it didn't even dent the heavy steel mesh.

Then Paul remembered the two-way radio Alex had given him. He pulled it out of his pocket and yelled desperately into it. 'Alex, can you hear me?'

They listened anxiously for a reply but heard only static.

'The cage must be blocking the radio signals,' Brian said.

Paul noticed a gas cylinder on a trolley at the other end of the cage. 'Dad, what's in that cylinder?'

'Liquid gas for low-temperature experiments. Why?'

Paul smiled. 'What happens when you reduce the temperature of metals?'

'They become brittle ...' He grinned as he understood Paul's plan. 'Yes! My son's a genius.'

'What are you talking about?' Riana asked.

'We can use the cold gas in the cylinder to weaken the cage,' Paul explained. 'Then we can break it.'

Brian eyed the expanse of electrified floor between them and the cylinder. 'How are we going to get to it?'

'Why don't we make it come to us?' Riana suggested. She picked up a small battery from a stack on the table. 'Give me your bootlaces,' she told Paul.

Brian watched in admiration as Riana fashioned a set of bolas out of the batteries and Paul's long bootlaces. She tied an electrical extension cord to the bolas, whirled them around her head and let them go. The bolas flew across the cage and wrapped around the handle of the trolley.

Brian clapped. 'Well done!' He and Paul carefully pulled on the extension cord and the trolley slowly rolled towards them on its rubber wheels.

Once the trolley was against the table, Brian turned the cylinder so that the valve pointed at the wall of the cage. He opened the valve and freezing white gas jetted out. After a few seconds, Brian closed the valve and the gas cleared. A large area of the mesh was white with frost. Brian smashed the wooden stool against the mesh and the frozen metal shattered, leaving a wide opening.

'Call Christine,' he told Paul once they were out of the cage. 'Tell her to get out of the house.'

Christine crowed with delight as she passed another car and started to close up on the race leader. She reached out to grab a handful of popcorn from a bowl beside her computer, then turned back to the game. She was so engrossed that she didn't hear the distant ringing of the telephone.

Alex stared at his science test paper. The questions weren't as hard as he had expected.

He looked over and saw Katrina smile at him. He smiled back. Suddenly, Paul's voice came from the bag at his feet. 'Alex, can you hear me? This is an emergency.'

Ms Gibson and the other students stared in surprise as Alex pulled the two-way radio from his bag and spoke into it. 'I read you, Paul. Where are you?'

'Alex, this is a test,' Ms Gibson said.

'Sssh!' Alex told her.

'Ashka's destroyed Dad's lab,' Paul babbled. 'She's after a new control unit for the power suit. It's in the bin in Dad's study. You've got to get it. It can make her fly. And get Christine out of the house.'

Ms Gibson stared incredulously as Alex got up from his desk. 'Alex!'

'Sorry, Miss. You heard Paul: it's an emergency.' He headed for the door. Katrina got up too.

'Katrina ...'

'We'll explain tomorrow, Miss.' She followed Alex out.

Alex and Katrina raced up the street towards

Paul's house and were relieved to see no sign of Ashka's car. As they hurried towards the front door, they heard a screech of brakes. They whirled round and saw Mrs Muggleton's car.

'Mum?' Katrina spluttered. 'How did you ... ?'

'The school called me. Get in the car.'

'But ...'

'I don't want to hear it! Do as you're told.'

'Sorry, Mum. I can't.'

Katrina ran to the front door of Paul's house. It was locked. Alex rang the doorbell. 'Christine!' he yelled. There was no reply.

Katrina grabbed a rock from the garden and Mrs Muggleton watched in stunned disbelief as her daughter smashed a pane of glass beside the door. Katrina reached inside and unlocked it.

'You look for the ... thingummyjig,' Alex said. 'I'll find Christine.'

They hurried into the house. Katrina raced up the stairs and burst into the study. She rummaged through the waste bin and found the flight control unit. As she stood up, she leaned on the keyboard of Brian's computer. The screen saver disappeared and Katrina found herself looking at the designs for the new power suit. She stared at the screen, fascinated by the possibilities of the marvellous device. Katrina saw a box of computer disks on the desk and smiled.

Alex raced into Christine's bedroom and the heavy popcorn bowl balanced above the door dropped onto his head. As he staggered, Christine burst out of the wardrobe and ran for the door. Alex grabbed her. 'Christine, it's me!'

'Alex? Why did you break in? What's happening?'

Paul and Riana braced themselves as Brian wrenched the steering wheel. The car screeched around a corner, narrowly missing a stop sign, and roared on. Katrina's voice came from the two-way radio. 'Paul, everything's fine. I've got the flight control unit and Alex has Christine.'

'Get out of the house,' Paul replied. 'Ashka will be there any second.'

'Roger. We'll meet at Alex's pl ...' Katrina's voice was smothered by static.

'Katrina?' Paul yelled into the radio. 'Katrina!'

There was only the sound of static.

'Ashka's there,' Paul said grimly. Brian floored the accelerator.

Katrina, Alex and Christine were heading for the stairs when lights started going on and off. Christine saw the look of fear on Alex's face. 'What's going on?'

'We'll tell you later.'

As Alex started pulling her down the stairs, the front door burst open and Ashka strode in. Christine smiled. 'Hello, Anna.'

'Bye,' Alex called. He and Katrina dragged Christine back up the stairs. Ashka ran after them.

Brian's car squealed to a halt on the footpath next to Ashka's.

'You two stay here,' he told Paul and Riana.

'But, Dad ...'

'Don't argue!' Brian jumped out of the car and ran towards the house.

'Mr Reynolds ...' Mrs Muggleton called,

getting out of her car. Brian ignored her and ran inside.

Alex, Katrina and Christine backed up against the desk in Brian's study. Ashka stood in the doorway, blocking their escape.

'Anna, what's going on?' Christine asked anxiously.

'Shut up!' Ashka snapped.

Alex put his arm around the frightened girl. 'It'll be OK.'

Katrina surreptitiously dropped the flight control unit on the floor and tried to kick it under the desk.

'Pick that up and give it to me,' Ashka demanded.

Katrina shook her head. Ashka fired a power-bolt and Brian's computer exploded. Christine screamed.

'You'd better do it,' Alex told Katrina.

Katrina picked up the unit and gingerly held it out. As Ashka reached for it, Brian burst into the study and tackled her. They crashed to the floor. The unit flew out of Ashka's hand and landed at Christine's feet.

'Chris, throw it out the window!' Brian yelled, trying to hold Ashka down. Ashka managed to energise the power suit. Electricity crackled over it and Brian was thrown across the room.

'Christine, give that to me,' Ashka said gently. 'I won't hurt you. I promise.'

Christine looked at her father, who lay moaning on the floor. Her eyes flitted to the window. Paul and Riana were in the garden below. As Ashka got up, Christine ran to the window. 'Paul!' she cried.

Paul and Riana looked up and saw Christine throw the control unit. It fell into some thick shrubs. Paul and Riana desperately started searching among the plants.

'I've got it!' Riana cried, just as Ashka burst out of the front door.

'Run!' Paul yelled. They raced away from the house.

Ashka raised her hand to fire a power-bolt.

'Katrina, no!' Mrs Muggleton called.

Ashka looked up. Alex and Katrina were pushing Brian's ruined computer out of the study window above her. She leaped aside and the heavy computer crashed to the ground at her feet. Ashka ran to the gate and saw Paul and Riana disappearing around a corner. She jumped into her car and roared after them.

An angry Mrs Muggleton was heading for the front door when Alex and Katrina helped Brian out of the house. 'I'm terribly sorry, Mr Reynolds,' she said, looking at the smashed computer. 'Katrina, have you gone completely out of your mind?'

'That woman's a Spellbinder, Mum,' Katrina explained. 'She's after Paul.'

'I've heard enough lies,' Mrs Muggleton snapped. 'Get in the car!'

'She's not lying,' Brian snapped back. 'Paul's in danger. Where did they go?'

Shocked by Brian's tone, Mrs Muggleton pointed up the street. Alex ran to Brian's car. 'Come on.'

Brian felt in his pockets. 'My keys are upstairs.'

'Mum, you'll have to drive.' Katrina dragged her bewildered mother towards her car.

Paul and Riana ran along the road beside the

container terminal. Ashka's car was gaining on them. Paul spotted a hole in the wire fence. 'Through there,' he panted.

As Riana scrambled through the narrow opening, she slipped and dropped the control unit. Paul scooped it up as Ashka's car screeched to a halt. Ashka leaped out and saw Paul and Riana disappear between a row of shipping containers. She energised the power suit and hurled a bolt at the fence, blasting a hole in the wire. She leaped through it and ran after them.

Paul and Riana crept between the stacks of containers, hoping to lose Ashka in the maze of passages. They reached an intersection and Paul signalled Riana to stop. They listened.

'Have we lost her?' Riana whispered.

'I think so.'

Paul peered around the corner. Ashka grabbed him and yanked him into the passage. The control unit flew from Paul's hand and fell to the ground. As Ashka bent to grab it, Riana dived past her. She grabbed the unit, rolled to her feet and ran down another passage. With a cry of rage, Ashka chased after her.

'There's her car!' Alex yelled.

Mrs Muggleton pulled up beside Ashka's car outside the container terminal. Brian leaped out and stared at the hole in the fence. The melted wire was still smoking. 'They must be in there. You stay here.' Brian hurried through the fence.

'Forget that,' Alex said. He and Katrina ran after him.

'Katrina, come back,' Mrs Muggleton shouted.

'I'll get her,' Christine said. She was gone before Mrs Muggleton could protest. Mrs Muggleton groaned and followed them.

Riana peered out from behind a row of containers. There were thirty metres of open space between her and the next row but beyond that was a gate which led out of the terminal. Riana was halfway across the space when Ashka's voice rang out: 'Riana!'

Riana looked around. Ashka was walking towards her. There was nothing between Riana and the nearest container but a pile of burning rubbish. She was trapped.

Riana stepped towards the rubbish and held the control unit over the flames. 'Get back or I'll burn it.'

Ashka stopped. 'Give it to me, Riana, and I won't harm your family.'

'Liar!'

Ashka touched a control on the power suit belt and raised her hand. To Riana's dismay, the control unit was pulled out of her hand by the suit's magnetic field. Ashka caught it.

'Thank you, Riana.' She began to fit the unit to the wrist of her suit.

Ashka was so intent on attaching the unit that she didn't notice the terminal's huge electro-magnets being slowly lowered towards her from the overhead crane. Riana looked up and saw Paul in the cab with Alex's father.

Riana stepped towards Ashka to distract her attention. 'I won't let you go back.'

Ashka laughed. 'How can you stop me?' She touched a button on the control unit and there was a hum of power. Ashka slowly rose into the air. 'You'll never see your family again, Riana,' she gloated.

Ashka touched the button again and rose

above the stacks of containers. She was still unaware of the electro-magnets that were descending towards her.

In the cab of the crane, Alex's father stared in amazement as Ashka hovered in mid-air. Paul's incredible story was true!

'Now!' Paul cried.

Stavros Katsonis hit a switch on the control panel.

Ashka's victorious grin faded as she was suddenly pulled upwards. She looked round and saw the electro-magnets above her. She jabbed desperately at the buttons on the control unit but the electro-magnets were too powerful and Ashka slammed into them. Energy crackled furiously around the suit as it burnt out and Ashka went limp. She dangled from the crane, held there by the magnetised power suit.

Paul climbed down from the crane and ran to Riana. 'We did it!' They hugged each other.

'Paul, are you alright?'

Paul looked round and saw his father running towards them, followed by Alex and Katrina. Christine and Mrs Muggleton were not far behind.

'What happened?' Katrina asked. 'Where's Ashka?'

Riana pointed up at Ashka, hanging motionless from the crane

'Tell your dad to let her down,' Paul told Alex.

Mrs Muggleton put her arm around Katrina as they watched Alex and his father tie up the struggling Ashka. 'I'm sorry I didn't believe you, Katrina. It all just sounded so ... so ...'

'It's OK, Mum,' Katrina said. 'I still don't really believe it myself.'

'I owe you an apology too, Alex,' Mrs Muggleton called.

Alex grinned as he tightened the rope on Ashka.

Brian looked up from the charred power suit. 'The circuits are all blown,' he told Paul and Riana. 'But if the powerstones are OK, I can build another suit.'

He opened the housing on the suit belt and carefully lifted out a powerstone. It crumbled and Brian watched in dismay as grey ash trickled through his fingers.

'Brian,' Ashka called, 'if you let me go free, I'll go back to my world and get more powerstones. Then we can build more suits and you'll be rich.'

'And let you rule the Spellbinders?' Paul said. 'No way!'

'What do you care about my world?' Ashka growled.

'We just don't like dictators,' Brian replied.

Christine looked from Ashka to her father. 'So what are we going to do with her?'

'Ashka belongs in my world,' Riana said. 'She must go back.'

The sun had just risen as Gryvon placed the Eyestone in position at the base of the Summoning Tower. He watched excitedly as energy flickered in the air and the doorway opened. Ashka stepped through.

'Now can we take over the Spellbinders?' Gryvon asked eagerly.

Then he realised that Ashka's hands were bound behind her back. He stared in shock as

Paul and Riana stepped through the doorway. Paul grinned at Gryvon. 'Surprise!'

'Help me, Gryvon,' Ashka roared.

Gryvon realised that Ashka's plan had failed and started to run towards Clayhill. Correon stepped out from behind a rock, blocking his path. Gryvon sank to his knees, defeated. Correon pulled him up and pushed him towards the Summoning Tower.

'Welcome back, Ashka,' Correon said. 'You two have an appointment with the Regents.'

'You promised I wouldn't get caught,' Gryvon wailed.

Ashka ignored him. 'Banish me if you like, Correon, but the Marauders will destroy the Spellbinders.'

'Really?' Correon replied with a smile. 'I was just with the Marauders, discussing the site for their new village. They seemed very happy.' Ashka scowled.

Paul and Riana looked at each other. There was nothing left to do but say goodbye.

'Life will be pretty quiet here without you,' Riana said.

'Not if I have anything to do with it,'

Correon declared. 'Riana, you've caused me a great deal of trouble.'

'Correon,' Paul protested, 'you don't ...'

Correon held up his hand. 'Quiet, Paul. Riana, you've continually disobeyed and contradicted me. You've been argumentative and disrespectful, and you're always asking questions that are none of your concern.'

Gryvon smirked at the shocked look on Riana's face.

'In fact,' Correon continued, 'you're just the sort of person I want as my new Apprentice.'

'No!' Gryvon wailed.

'But I'm not clever enough,' Riana objected.

'Do you think Gryvon is cleverer than you?' Paul asked.

Riana chuckled. 'I'll do it ... I mean, I would be honoured, Regent.' She bowed to Correon.

'Great,' Paul exclaimed. 'You'll get to live in the castle.'

'Whenever you come back, you can visit us,' Correon offered.

'I don't think that's such a good idea. If people from my world found out about the doorway and started coming here, who knows what would happen.'

Riana's eyes lit up. 'We'd have TV.'

'And developers,' Paul added. 'They'd turn your land into a theme park: Spellbinder World. Tours of the castle and rides in the flying ship. You wouldn't be able to afford to live here.'

'He's right, Regent,' Riana said. 'His world would take over ours. His people are too clever.'

Correon nodded. 'Then we must make our people clever. We have to share the Spellbinders' knowledge.'

'Don't be a fool,' Ashka snapped. 'The Spellbinders will lose their power.'

'Things have to change,' Correon replied.

'I'd better go,' Paul said. 'I don't want Dad getting worried again.'

Correon put his hand on Paul's shoulder. 'Thank you, Paul. Our world owes you a great deal.'

Paul shook Correon's hand, then turned to Riana. 'Do you think you can live without me?' he asked with a smile.

'I'll try.' She gave Paul a hug. He held her tightly for a moment then moved towards the doorway.

'I'll always be here if you need me,' Riana called.

Paul gave a final wave and disappeared through the doorway. Correon turned to Riana. 'Apprentice, remove the Eyestone.'

Paul stood with his father, watching through the rippling curtain of energy as Riana lifted the Eyestone from the dish.

'It's a pity to close it,' Brian said. 'How many other parallel worlds might there be?'

The doorway disappeared. Power stopped crackling around the cable above their heads and for a moment there was silence. Then the normal sounds of the bush returned. It was as if the doorway had never existed.

'What will happen to Ashka?' Christine asked.

'That's up to Correon and the other Regents to decide,' Paul answered.

'Whatever it is,' Katrina said, 'I hope it's really unpleasant.'

'We'd better get the cable down before something else happens,' Alex suggested. He and Brian got to work.

Paul gazed sadly at the place where the doorway had been.

'I'll miss her too,' Christine said.

Paul put his arm around his sister and smiled.

Paul and Alex walked through the schoolyard, kicking a soccer ball between them. It was just another lunchtime.

'I wish I'd had a chance to try out that power suit,' Paul said regretfully. 'Imagine being able to fly.'

'Imagine what people would pay for one,' Alex said.

'We'll never know. Ashka destroyed all Dad's notes.'

They were passing the science laboratory when Katrina leaned out of the window. 'Hey, you two. Get in here.'

'Why?' Alex asked.

'Just do it.'

She disappeared. Paul and Alex shrugged at each other and went inside. They found Katrina in front of a computer.

'You know we're not supposed to be in here at lunchtime,' Paul reminded her.

'Not even for this?' Smiling mysteriously, Katrina slotted a disk into the computer. She pressed a key and a diagram of the new power suit appeared on the screen.

'How did you get that?' Paul asked in amazement. 'Ashka destroyed everything.'

Katrina grinned. 'I copied your Dad's computer files before she arrived.'

'All of them?' Paul asked.

'Every one.'

Paul, Alex and Katrina stared at the computer screen, their eyes gleaming with excitement.

'Are you guys thinking what I'm thinking?' Paul asked.

The three friends grinned at each other. Maybe the adventure wasn't over.

THE END

SPILLING THE MAGIC

Stephen Moore

Staying with boring relatives, life looks bleak for Billy and Mary until they find . . .

A strange book of spells.

Whisked into the mysterious, multi-coloured world of Murn they find a world on its last legs.

A world knee-deep in spilt magic.

Even with the help of flying pigs and a vegetarian dragon, can they put the magic back where it belongs?

THE HOUSE OF BIRDS

Jenny Jones

Ominously overshadowing the village, Pelham Hall stands apart. Strange shrieks are heard from inside its walls.

Masked raiders thunder through the streets on huge black stallions. Their nightly catch is village children.

Harriet, orphaned and abandoned, sees her friends disappear, one by one.

Will she be next . . . ?

DAUGHTER OF STORMS

Louise Cooper

Born in a supernatural storm, under a crimson sun, Shar is destined for the Sisterhood.

Innocent of the power she controls, Shar is of great value to others – who patiently lie waiting for such a soul.

But as Shar begins to realise her gift, the terror begins . . .

In a land where the gods of Order and Chaos rule – a deadly power is rising. Can Shar summon the elements to become the Dark Caller?